序　言

　　「英文趣味閱讀測驗」（ *Readings for Fun* ）編輯的目的，在提供讀者豐富有趣的閱讀材料，讓您經由輕鬆的閱讀提高英文能力，並培養對英文的興趣。

　　本書主要特色如下：

◆輕薄短小，趣味橫溢——本書所選文章，用字淺顯，精巧迷你，不到五分鐘就能讀完一篇。內容幽默風趣，您會忍不住一篇接一篇地讀下去，馬上獲得成就感，建立自信心。

♥取材廣泛，編排明朗——本書涵括：解頤短文、生活小品、奇風異俗、名人軼聞……包羅萬象，不勝枚舉；配合簡單清爽的版面編排、詳盡的注解和流暢的翻譯，使您的閱讀成為一種享受。

♣啓發式習題，激發閱讀潛力——本書每篇都附精選習題，可測驗您的理解力（ *comprehension* ），幫您掌握文章重點，突破閱讀盲點（ *blind spot* ）！

♠由淺入深，漸入佳境——本書共分三級，只要您具備基本的英文程度，就能隨著本書，逐步進入多彩多姿的閱讀領域，體會漸入佳境的奇妙感受。

　　本書雖經多次審慎校閱，惟恐尚有疏失之處，切盼各界先進不吝批評指正。

編者　謹識

Editorial Staff

- **企劃・編著** / 陳瑠琍
- **英文撰稿** / David Bell
- **校訂**

    劉　毅・陳怡平・陳威如・王慶銘・王怡華
    許碧珍・劉馨君・林順隆

- **校閱**

    Nick Veitch・Francesca A. Evans
    Joanne Beckett・Thomas Denean
    Stacy Schultz・Jeffrey R. Carr
    David M. Quesenberry・Chris Virani
    Kirk Kofford・林佩汀・陳麒永

- **封面設計** / 張鳳儀
- **插畫** / 張端懿・蘇淑玲
- **版面設計** / 張鳳儀
- **版面構成** / 蘇淑玲・張端懿・林新益
- **打字**

    黃淑貞・倪秀梅・蘇淑玲・吳秋香・徐湘君

CONTENTS

1. The Shopping List／購物單 ……………………… 2

2. The Fight／打架 …………………………………… 4

3. Don't Put All Your Eggs in One Basket／
別把蛋放在同一個籃子裏 ……………… 6

4. Ignorance Is Bliss／無知便是福 ……………… 8

5. A Clever Solution／聰明的解釋 ……………… 10

6. The Measure of Success／成功的標準 ……… 12

7. A Truthful Letter／一封實話實說的信 ……… 14

8. A Trick That Backfired／聰明反被聰明誤 …… 16

9. An Easy Choice／必然的選擇 ………………… 18

10. The Merry Widows／快樂的寡婦 …………… 20

11. Flashes of Insight／靈機一動 ……………… 22

12. A Slow Learner／學習遲鈍 ………………… 24

13. A Man in a Hurry／趕時間的人 …………… 26

14. World War Ⅳ／第四次世界大戰 …………… 28

15. A Survivor／生存者 ………………………… 30

Dear Ann Landers — Unfair Interference
親愛的安・蘭德絲 — 不公平的干涉 ……… 32

16. An April Fool's Trick／愚人節的花招 ……… 34

17. Smoking Patterns of Teenagers／
青少年的抽煙模式 …………………………… 36

18. Economy — Not Always the Best Policy /
節儉並非上策 ……………………………… **38**

19. A Practical Student / 重實際的學生 ………… **40**

20. A Hesitant General / 猶豫不決的將軍 ……… **42**

21. A Wise Grandmother / 聰明的祖母 ………… **44**

22. Valuable Salt / 珍貴的鹽 …………………… **46**

23. Alienation and Aging / 疏遠與老化 ………… **48**

24. A Terrifying Moment / 可怕的時刻 ………… **50**

25. Not That Kind of Painter ! /
是畫家，不是油漆匠！ ………………………… **52**

26. The IRS Strikes Again / 國稅局的老把戲 …… **54**

27. Never Satisfied / 毫不知足 ………………… **56**

28. A Playboy / 花花公子 ……………………… **58**

29. A Man of Principle / 有原則的人 …………… **60**

30. The Vital Role of Risk / 冒險的重要性 ……… **62**

Dear Abby — Gratitude
親愛的艾比—感恩 …………………………… **64**

31. Deciphering Faces / 讀人們的臉 …………… **66**

32. Sex Discrimination / 性別歧視 …………… **68**

33. Transmission of Culture / 文化的薪傳 ……… **70**

34. The Greatest Regret / 最深的懊悔 ………… **72**

35. Emotions : Express, Don't Repress /
情緒要表達，不要壓抑 ……………………… **74**

36. Outwitted / 青出於藍 ……………………… **76**

37. Changing Attitudes Toward Children /
改變管教小孩的態度 ………………………… **78**

38. The Truth About Exercise / 運動的眞義 …… **80**

39. Jumping to Conclusions / 遽下斷語 ……… **82**

40. Two Views of Marriage /
　　對婚姻的兩種看法 ················· 84

41. An Unrecognized Vice / 不爲人知的惡習 ······· 86

42. Appreciating Distance / 珍惜距離 ············· 88

43. That's Perfect / 太完美了 ············· 90

44. The Danger of Sensationalism /
　　煽情的危險 ················· 92

45. An Encouraging Prediction /
　　激勵人心的預言 ················· 94

Dear Ann Landers — Overcoming a Phobia
親愛的安・蘭德絲 — 克服恐懼症 ················· 96

46. Legal Aid / 法律援助 ············· 98

47. Retiring from Life / 從生命中退休 ············· 100

48. How Italy Rediscovered Her Past /
　　義大利的文藝復興 ················· 102

49. Speak Up! / 大聲說出來！ ············· 104

50. Save the Whales / 拯救鯨魚 ············· 106

51. A Polite Request / 客氣的要求 ············· 108

52. On Edge / 如臨深淵 ············· 110

53. Save the Sharks / 拯救鯊魚 ············· 112

54. The Mind as a Laboratory / 頭腦實驗室 ······ 114

55. Wake Them Up / 叫醒他們 ············· 116

56. A Hidden Cause of Accidents /
　　意外事件的隱形肇因 ················· 118

57. Choosing a Resort / 選擇度假地點 ············· 120

58. Theater as Catharsis / 劇場的淨化作用 ······· 122

59. Two National Characters /
　　有其國必有其民 ················· 124

60. Reducing Anxiety／減少焦慮 ……………… **126**

Dear Ann Landers — A Pleasant Problem
親愛的安・蘭德絲 — 令人愉快的難題 …………… **128**

61. A Willful Misunderstanding／
蓄意的誤解 ……………………………… **130**

62. Practice Without Pressure／
在沒有壓力之下練習 …………………… **132**

63. That's Thin Enough／夠瘦了 ……… **134**

64. Spare the Rod…?／不打就…? …………… **136**

65. A Practical Suggestion／實際的建議 ……… **138**

66. Training Elephants／訓練大象 …………… **140**

67. Watch Closely!／仔細觀察! ………………… **142**

68. Over-Motivation／動機過強 …………… **144**

69. Mayan Mathematics／馬雅人的數學 ……… **146**

70. A Heroic Nurse／勇敢的護士 …………… **148**

71. The Disco-Dancing Parliamentarian／
跳迪斯可的國會議員 …………………… **150**

72. Irrational Fears／非理性的恐懼 ………… **152**

73. Modern Attitudes Toward Marriage／
現代人對婚姻的態度 …………………… **154**

74. Social Maturity／成熟的社會人 …………… **156**

75. Our Works Reveal What Our Masks Conceal／
觀其事知其人 …………………………… **158**

Dear Ann Landers — Controversy Over
Breast-Feeding
親愛的安・蘭德絲 — 對當衆餵母奶的爭議 …… **160**

＊內文翻譯・習題解答 …………………… **163**

To see a world in a grain of sand
And a heaven in a wild flower,
Hold infinity in the palm of your hand
And eternity in an hour.

— William Blake

1 The Shopping List

Mrs. Black was having a lot of trouble with her skin, so she went to her doctor about it. He sent her to the local hospital for some tests, and telephoned her the next morning to give her a list of the things that he thought she should not eat, as any of them might be the cause of her skin trouble. Mrs. Black carefully wrote all the things down on a piece of paper, which she then left beside the telephone while she went out to a ladies' meeting.

When she got back home two hours later, she found her husband waiting for her. "Hullo, dear," he said, "I have done all your shopping for you." "Done all my shopping?" she asked in surprise. "But how did you know what I wanted?" "I found your shopping list beside the telephone," answered her husband. Of course, Mrs. Black had to tell him that he had bought all the things_____.

** *have trouble with* 因~而煩惱　　*send A to B for C* 送A去B做C
skin trouble 皮膚病　　**hullo**〔hə'lo, 'hʌlo〕*interj.* 哈囉（＝*hello*）

❖ Comprehension ❖

1. Which of the following best completes the last sentence ?

   (A) she really liked to eat
   (B) that were much too expensive
   (C) the doctor did not allow her to eat
   (D) her husband really liked to eat

2. Mrs. Black went to the local hospital_____ .

   (A) to be examined by her doctor
   (B) for some tests
   (C) for treatment of her skin trouble
   (D) because her husband suggested it

3. Mrs. Black made a list of_____ .

   (A) foods her doctor said not to eat
   (B) telephone numbers she often dialed
   (C) the results of her skin tests
   (D) foods she wanted her husband to buy

4. Mr. Black's attempt to help his wife with the shopping_____ .

   (A) made her very pleased
   (B) was actually very helpful
   (C) made her feel guilty
   (D) was unsuccessful

** **treatment** 〔'tritmənt〕 *n.* 治療
   guilty 〔'gɪltɪ〕 *adj.* 心虛的；自覺有罪的

The Fight

Late one night, Nasreddin was woken up by two men fighting in the street. As Nasreddin loved nothing better than to watch a fight, he opened his window and looked out, but when they saw him watching them, they went round the corner of the house. Nasreddin did not want to miss anything, but, as it was a cold night, he wrapped himself in a blanket before he went out.

The two men were still shouting and struggling. Nasreddin went closer to them, but as soon as he was within reach, they seized his blanket and ran away. Nasreddin was too old to run after them, so he could do nothing but go sadly back to bed.

" Well, " said his wife. "＿＿＿＿＿＿ "

" It seems that they were fighting about my blanket," answered Nasreddin, " because as soon as they got it, their quarrel ended. "

** wrap〔ræp〕v. 包；裹   blanket〔'blæŋkɪt〕n. 毛毯
struggle〔'strʌɡḷ〕vi. 搏鬥   *within reach* 在手可以達到的地方

❖ Comprehension ❖

1. Which sentence best fits in the blank?
   (A) Where have you been tonight?
   (B) What were they fighting about?
   (C) You seem very cold and sad.
   (D) Hurry up and come to bed.

2. Nasreddin was woken up by_____.
   (A) his wife
   (B) the fight
   (C) a rooster
   (D) his alarm clock

3. The two men were probably_____.
   (A) angry with each other
   (B) angry with Nasreddin
   (C) only pretending to fight
   (D) the friends of Nasreddin

4. From this story it seems that_____.
   (A) Nasreddin was somewhat foolish
   (B) Nasreddin was afraid of fighting
   (C) fighting is dangerous
   (D) Nasreddin was angry with his wife

** *run after* 追   quarrel〔'kwɔrəl〕*n.* 爭吵
   rooster〔'rustɚ〕*n.* 公雞
   pretend〔prɪ'tɛnd〕*v.* 假裝
   somewhat〔'sʌm,hwɑt〕*adv.* 稍微;有點

③ Don't Put All Your Eggs in One Basket

A friend of mine, once noticing the haphazard way in which I kept paper money in my various pockets, much of it lost among a medley of letters and other documents in my breast pocket, said to me : " You have no sense about money. You don't know how to keep it, " and presented me with a note-case, when I was on the eve of going abroad. I put all my paper money into the note-case, feeling that I was a practical man at last. Within a week, unfortunately, a still more practical pickpocket managed to get hold of the note-case and robbed me of a far larger sum than any pickpocket had ever succeeded in taking from me in my more unpractical days.

** haphazard〔͵hæpˊhæzəd〕 *adj.* 隨便的   **paper money** 紙鈔
medley〔ˊmɛdlɪ〕 *n.* 混雜   **document**〔ˊdɑkjəmənt〕 *n.* 文件
present *A with B* 贈送A（人）B（物）
note-case〔ˊnot͵kes〕 *n.* 皮夾子
practical〔ˊpræktɪkl̩〕 *adj.* 講求實際的

◈ Comprehension ◈

1. The writer's friend gave him _____ .

    (A) some money

    (B) a kind of purse

    (C) an important letter

    (D) some documents

2. The writer was given a present _____ .

    (A) while he was travelling

    (B) because he asked for one

    (C) before he went abroad

    (D) after he returned from abroad

3. The note-case was taken by_____ .

    (A) the bank

    (B) a thief

    (C) the government

    (D) the friend

4. The writer was better off_____ .

    (A) with the note-case

    (B) without money

    (C) after the theft

    (D) being unpractical

** **pickpocket** 〔'pɪk,pɑkɪt〕 *n.* 扒手   ***get hold of*** 獲得
be better off 處境更好

Ignorance Is Bliss

　　It would seem obvious that a sharpsighted hen would be much better off than a short-sighted hen, for good vision is better than poor vision. But this may not always be so.

　　Some grain is placed behind a wiregrating and a hen is placed in front of the grating. The sharp-sighted hen sees the grain at once and goes directly towards it. She is stopped by the grating, but so clear and beckoning is the sight of the grain that she spends all her time trying

───────── .

** bliss〔blɪs〕n. 福氣
sharp-sighted〔'ʃɑrp'saɪtɪd〕adj. 視覺敏銳的（↔ short-sighted 近視的）
be better off 境遇更好　　vision〔'vɪʒən〕n. 視力
wiregrating〔'waɪr,gretɪŋ〕n. 鐵絲網
beckon〔'bɛkən〕v. 招手　　get through 通過
take advantage of 利用　　fruitless〔'frutlɪs〕adj. 徒勞的
It never rains but it pours. 一下雨就是傾盆而降。
The early bird catches the worm. 早起的鳥兒有蟲吃。

❖ Comprehension ❖

1. Which of the following best completes the last sentence ?
   (A) to get rid of the grain
   (B) to find the grain
   (C) to get through the grating
   (D) to take advantage of a short-sighted hen

2. The main idea of the paragraph is_____.
   (A) how stupid a short-sighted hen is
   (B) how a hen gets grain
   (C) the disadvantage of a sharp-sighted hen
   (D) the disadvantage of a short-sighted hen

3. Which is true, according to the paragraph ?
   (A) A hen is usually sharp-sighted.
   (B) A hen knows how to get the grain behind a wire-grating.
   (C) Even a sharp-sighted hen fails to see the grain nearby.
   (D) Sometimes sharp-sighted hens make fruitless efforts.

4. Which proverb is supported by the story ?
   (A) Everything comes to those who wait.
   (B) It never rains but it pours.
   (C) The early bird catches the worm.
   (D) Knowledge sometimes causes unnecessary troubles.

A Clever Solution

The manager of a small building company was very surprised to get a bill for two white mice which one of his workmen had bought. He asked the workman why he had had the bill sent to the company.

" Well, " the workman answered, " you remember the house we were repairing? We had to put some new electric wiring through a pipe thirty feet long and about an inch across which had four big bends in it. None of us could think how to do this until I had a good idea. I went and bought two white mice, one male and the other female. Then I tied a thread to the male mouse, while Bill held the female mouse at the other end. When the male mouse heard the female mouse's squeaks, he rushed along the pipe to help her. As he ran through the pipe he pulled the thread behind him. It was then quite easy for us to tie one end of the thread to the electric wires and pull them through the pipe. "

The manager paid the bill for the white mice.

❖ Comprehension ❖

1. The mice were_____.
   - (A) both female
   - (B) killed by a cat
   - (C) extremely expensive
   - (D) useful to the workmen

2. The workmen had a problem_____.
   - (A) passing a wire through a long pipe
   - (B) keeping the mice apart
   - (C) finding a pair of mice
   - (D) caused by a cat

3. At the end of the story the manager was_____.
   - (A) angry with the workman
   - (B) tricked by the workman
   - (C) satisfied
   - (D) persuaded to buy more mice

4. The workman in the story was_____.
   - (A) lazy
   - (B) stupid
   - (C) creative
   - (D) dishonest

** solution〔sə'luʃən〕*n.* （問題等的）解釋；說明
electric wiring〔集合用法〕電線線路　　bend〔bend〕*n.* 轉彎
tie A to B 把A綁在B上　　squeak〔skwik〕*n.* （老鼠的）吱吱叫聲
trick〔trɪk〕*v.* 欺騙　　persuade〔pəˈswed〕*v.* 說服

6

The Measure of Success

Americans feel proud of themselves for working hard, but they feel equally proud of themselves when they sit and do nothing over weekends.

As a matter of fact some Americans measure success in terms of the length and frequency of their vacations. The man who gets a month's vacation each year considers himself more successful than the man who gets two weeks. Many people become teachers because teachers get a three-month vacation every year.

In brief, the less work some Americans do, the more _____ they consider themselves.

** **measure**〔ˊmɛʒɚ〕 *n.* （評價、判斷等的）標準
　feel proud of 以～爲傲　　*in terms of* 由～的觀點
　frequency〔ˊfrikwənsɪ〕 *n.* 次數；頻繁　　*in brief* 簡言之
　social status 社會地位　　**environment**〔ɪnˊvaɪrənmənt〕 *n.* 環境
　troublesome〔ˊtrʌblsəm〕 *adj.* 麻煩的
　claim〔klem〕 *n.* 聲言；主張

❖ Comprehension ❖

1. Frequency of vacations means _____ .
   - (A) how long they last
   - (B) how often they occur
   - (C) how much fun they are
   - (D) how much they cost

2. According to this passage, many people become teachers because of _____ .
   - (A) the good salary
   - (B) the high social status
   - (C) the long vacations
   - (D) the pleasant working environment

3. What word is most suitable for the blank?
   - (A) lazy
   - (B) troublesome
   - (C) successful
   - (D) unfortunate

4. Which of the following does NOT support the author's claim?
   - (A) Many Americans choose to retire early.
   - (B) Many workers take long lunch breaks.
   - (C) Women fight for the right to work.
   - (D) Labor-saving devices are very popular.

7 A Truthful Letter

Matthew Hobbs was sixteen years old. He had been at the same school for five years, and he had always been a very bad pupil. He was lazy, he fought with other pupils, he was rude to the teachers, and he did not obey the rules of the school. His headmaster_____, but he was never successful — and the worst thing was that, as Matthew grew older, he was a bad influence on the younger boys.

Then at last Matthew left school. He tried to get a job with a big company, and the manager wrote to the headmaster to find out what he could say about Matthew. The headmaster wanted to be honest, but he also did not want to be too hard, so he wrote, " If you can get Matthew Hobbs to work for you, you will be very lucky. "

** **rude**〔rud〕*adj.* 無禮的
headmaster〔'hɛd'mæstɚ〕*n.* 校長（ *cf.* headmistress 女校長 ）
hard〔hɑrd〕*adj.* 刻薄的　　**behave**〔bɪ'hev〕*v.* 行爲；舉動
disobedient〔,dɪsə'bidɪənt〕*adj.* 不服從的
be qualified for 能適任；有資格　　**interpret**〔ɪn'tɝprɪt〕*v.* 解釋

❖ Comprehension ❖

1. Which of the following best fits in the blank ?
   (A) was basically fond of Matthew
   (B) tried to make him work and behave better
   (C) wrote an angry letter to Matthew's parents one day
   (D) did not like to punish his students

2. According to the passage, what was the worst thing about Matthew ?
   (A) He was lazy.
   (B) He fought with others.
   (C) He was rude and disobedient.
   (D) He was a bad influence.

3. What did the headmaster mean by the last line ?
   (A) Matthew Hobbs is very lazy and unlikely to work.
   (B) It would be fortunate for that company to have Matthew as an employee.
   (C) Matthew has had good luck.
   (D) Matthew is qualified for that particular kind of job.

4. How would the manager interpret the last line ?
   (A) Matthew is lucky to be employed.
   (B) It would be fortunate for that company to have Matthew as an employee.
   (C) Matthew tends to have good luck.
   (D) Matthew isn't qualified for that particular kind of job.

8

A Trick That Backfired

One day a farmer, who was well known in his village as a very mean man, said, "I will give three meals and twenty-five pence to anyone who is willing to do a day's work for me." This offer was accepted by a hungry tramp, who was more interested in the meals than the money. "You can have your breakfast first," said the farmer, "and then you can start work." After the farmer had given him a very small breakfast, he said, "Now you can have your lunch. This will save us a lot of time." The tramp agreed, and ate a poor lunch. Then the farmer said, "What would you say to having dinner also while you are about it?"

When the tramp had finished his dinner the farmer looked very pleased and said, "Now you can do a long day's work." "Sorry," said the tramp as he rose to leave, "I never work after dinner!"

** **backfire**〔'bæk,faɪr〕*vi.* 招致與預期相反的後果
　　mean〔min〕*adj.* 小氣的　　**pence**〔pɛns〕*n.* 辨士（penny 的複數）

❖ Comprehension ❖

1. In this case, "mean" means _____.
   (A) cruel   (B) miserly
   (C) average   (D) rough

2. The tramp decided to work for the farmer because
   _____.
   (A) he was very hungry
   (B) he was not interested in the money
   (C) he liked working
   (D) the farmer was well known as a mean man

⁂3. "While you are about it" means_____.
   (A) while you are working
   (B) if you are still hungry
   (C) while you are at my farm
   (D) while you are eating

4. The tramp ate _____.
   (A) all his meals at the wrong time of day
   (B) all his meals at the right time of day
   (C) only one of his meals at the right time of day
   (D) only one of his meals at the wrong time of day

** **offer**〔'ɔfɚ, 'ɑfɚ〕 *n.* 提議   **tramp**〔træmp〕 *n.* 流浪漢
   What would you say to V-ing? ~怎麼樣?要不要~?(=*How about* ~?)
   be about 從事(= *be engaged in*)
   miserly〔'maɪzɚlɪ〕 *adj.* 吝嗇的

9 An Easy Choice

One day, the naval police in one big seaport received an urgent telephone call from a bar in the town. The barman said that a big sailor had got drunk and was breaking the furniture in the bar. The petty officer who was in charge of the naval police guard that evening said that he would come immediately. Now, petty officers who had to go and deal with sailors who were violently drunk usually chose the biggest naval policeman they could find to go with them. But this particular petty officer did not do this. Instead, he chose _____ to go to the bar with him and arrest the sailor who was breaking the furniture.

Another petty officer said to him, "Why don't you take a big man with you? You may have to fight the sailor who is drunk." "Yes, you are quite right," answered the petty officer of the guard. "But if you saw two policemen coming to arrest you, and one of them was much smaller than the other, which one would you attack?"

** **naval** 〔'nevļ〕 *adj.* 海軍的　　**urgent** 〔'ɜdʒənt〕 *adj.* 緊急的

❖ Comprehension ❖

1. The first petty officer _____.

   (A) had been drinking
   (B) was in charge of the naval police
   (C) was a big man   (D) broke the furniture

2. Which of the following fits in the blank?

   (A) the smallest, weakest-looking man he could find
   (B) an exceptionally big and strong officer
   (C) a female officer   (D) not to ask anyone

3. The second petty officer was surprised because

   _____.

   (A) the first petty officer chose a small man
   (B) the sailor wasn't really very drunk
   (C) so much furniture had been broken
   (D) sailors very rarely caused trouble

4. What was the first petty officer going to do to the man causing trouble in the bar?

   (A) attack him   (B) draft him into the navy
   (C) get him drunk   (D) arrest him

** **barman**〔'bɑrmən〕 *n.* 〔英〕酒吧侍者(=〔美〕*bartender*)
   petty officer 海軍上士   *in charge of* 負責
   guard〔gɑrd〕*n.* 看守   *deal with* 對付
   violently〔'vaɪələntlɪ〕*adv.* 厲害地
   particular〔pə'tɪkjələ〕*adj.* 特別的   **arrest**〔ə'rɛst〕*v.* 逮捕
   draft〔dræft〕*v.* 徵募   **navy**〔'nevɪ〕*n.* 海軍

10 The Merry Widows

Mr. Brown was at the theater. He found himself in the middle of a group of American ladies, some of them middle-aged and some quite old. Before the curtain went up on the play, they all talked and joked a lot together.

After the first act of the play, one lady apologized to Mr. Brown for the noisiness of her friends. He answered that he was very glad to see American ladies so obviously enjoying their visit to England. Mr. Brown's neighbor explained what they were doing there.

"You know, I have known these ladies all my life," she said. "They have all lost their husbands, and call themselves the Merry Widows. They go abroad every summer for a month or two and have a lot of fun. I had wanted to join their club for a long time, but I didn't qualify for membership until the spring of this year."

** **widow**〔'wɪdo〕 *n.* 寡婦　　**curtain**〔'kɝtn̩〕 *n.* （舞台上的）幕
act〔ækt〕 *n.* （戲的）一幕　　**apologize**〔ə'pɑlə,dʒaɪz〕 *v.* 道歉

❖ Comprehension ❖

1. Each of the women had a husband who_____.
   (A) visited England
   (B) visited America
   (C) died
   (D) enjoyed watching plays

2. Mr. Brown's conversation with the woman was
   _____.
   (A) friendly
   (B) angry
   (C) annoying the audience
   (D) related to the play

3. That spring, the _____.
   (A) Merry Widows went abroad
   (B) women formed a club
   (C) woman's husband died
   (D) play was performed in America

4. The woman qualified for membership by_____.
   (A) travelling to England
   (B) going to the theater
   (C) becoming a widow
   (D) joining the club

** *qualify for* 具備~資格 **membership**〔'mɛmbɚ,ʃɪp〕 *n.* 會員資格
annoy〔ə'nɔɪ〕 *v.* 妨害；騷擾

11

Flashes of Insight

There are few experiences quite so satisfactory as getting a good idea.

You've had a problem, you've thought about it till you were tired, forgotten it and perhaps slept on it, and then flash! When you weren't thinking about it, suddenly the answer has come to you, as a gift from the gods. You're pleased with it, and feel good. It may not be right, but at least you can try it out.

Of course all ideas don't come like that, but the interesting thing is that so many do, particularly the most important ones. They burst into the mind, glowing with the heat of creation.

** **flash**〔flæʃ〕 *n.*, *v.* 閃現　　**insight**〔'ɪn,saɪt〕 *n.* 洞察力；見識
satisfactory〔,sætɪs'fæktərɪ〕 *adj.* 令人滿意的
sleep on sth. 把（問題等）留待第二天解決　　***try out*** 徹底試驗
burst into 突然進入　　**glow**〔glo〕 *v.* 燃燒

❖ Comprehension ❖

1. " Slept on it" means _____ .
   (A) continued to sleep for a better solution
   (B) postponed the solution to the problem to the next day
   (C) had a good dream about the problem
   (D) found the solution to the problem in a dream

2. Ideas like this_____ .
   (A) come when you're tired
   (B) are always right
   (C) are satisfactory but not good
   (D) come when you're not thinking about them

3. _____ good ideas come this way.
   (A) All
   (B) Most
   (C) Many
   (D) A few

4. What does "so many do" mean in this passage ?
   (A) Interesting ideas always turn out to be right.
   (B) Many ideas often come suddenly.
   (C) Many interesting things happen suddenly.
   (D) Many important ideas suddenly come from the gods.

** solution〔sə'luʃən〕 *n.* (問題等的) 解決   *turn out* 結果是～

12 A Slow Learner

I persuaded my uncle to let me have a bicycle at the beginning of the summer holidays. My aunt was against it, saying I should only break my neck, but she at last yielded to my persistence. I ordered it before school broke up, and a few days later I was the owner of a beautiful new bicycle.

I was determined to learn to ride it by myself, and chaps at school had told me that they had learned in half an hour. I tried and tried, and at last came to the conclusion that I was abnormally stupid, but even after my pride was sufficiently humbled for me to allow the gardener to hold me up, I seemed at the end of the first morning no nearer to being able to get on by myself than at the beginning.

** persuade〔pə'swed〕v. 說服　　yield to 屈服；讓步
persistence〔pə'sɪstəns〕n. 堅持　　break up 結束
determine〔dɪ'tɜmɪn〕v. 決定　　chap〔tʃæp〕n. 人；傢伙
abnormally〔æb'nɔrmḷɪ〕adv. 異常地
sufficiently〔sə'fɪʃəntlɪ〕adv. 充分地　　humble〔'hʌmbḷ〕v. 貶低
hold up 扶住

❖ Comprehension ❖

1. The boy's uncle gave him _____.

   (A) a holiday   (B) a bicycle

   (C) some pocket money   (D) some help

2. When the boy said that he wanted to ride a bicycle,
   _____.

   (A) his aunt encouraged him to try

   (B) his friends told him it was easy

   (C) his uncle refused to allow it

   (D) his friend sold him his new bicycle

3. Which is true, according to the passage above?

   (A) The boy wanted to ride a bicycle and finally learned how.

   (B) The boy wanted to teach himself to ride the bicycle, but it wasn't easy.

   (C) The gardener decided to teach the boy how to ride the bicycle.

   (D) In the end, the boy decided to give up trying to ride the bicycle.

4. The boy thought he was "abnormally stupid" because he _____.

   (A) took longer than half an hour to learn to ride

   (B) let the gardener hold him up

   (C) almost broke his neck

   (D) had bought the bicycle

13 A Man in a Hurry

A police officer in a small town stopped a motorist who was speeding down Main Street. "But, officer," the man began, " I can explain — "

" Just be quiet, " snapped the officer. " I'm going to let you calm down while waiting in jail until the chief gets back. "

"But, officer, I just wanted to say — "

"And I said to keep quiet! You're going to jail!" A few hours later the officer looked in on his prisoner and said, "Lucky for you that the chief's at his daughter's wedding. He'll be in a good mood when he gets back. "

"Don't count on it," answered the fellow in the cell. " I'm the groom. "

** motorist〔'motərɪst〕 *n.* 開汽車的人　　**speed**〔spid〕*v.* 超速行駛
snap〔snæp〕*v.* 吼著說　　*calm down* 冷靜下來
chief〔tʃif〕*n.* 長官　　*look in on* 探望
prisoner〔'prɪznɚ, 'prɪznɚ〕*n.* 犯人

◆ Comprehension ◆

1. _____ was stopped on Main Street.

    (A) A police officer

    (B) The police chief

    (C) The police chief's daughter

    (D) The police chief's daughter's fiancé

2. Why was the motorist stopped?

    (A) He was driving too fast.

    (B) He was rude to the officer.

    (C) He was late for the wedding.

    (D) He had escaped from jail.

3. What is meant by the phrase "Don't count on it"?

    (A) Sooner than you think.

    (B) Not necessarily.

    (C) Too many to be counted.

    (D) Don't expect any medals.

4. Who was going to marry the motorist?

    (A) the police officer

    (B) the police chief

    (C) the police chief's daughter

    (D) the police chief's daughter's fiancé

** **wedding**〔'wɛdɪŋ〕 *n.* 婚禮   **mood**〔mud〕 *n.* 心情
count on 指望；依賴   **cell**〔sɛl〕 *n.* 小囚房
groom〔grum〕 *n.* 新郎   **fiancé**〔ˌfiən'se〕 *n.* 未婚夫

World War Ⅳ

A grim joke, current just after the end of World War Ⅱ, consisted in the remark that, whereas the most important weapon of the next war would be the atom bomb, the most important weapon of the war after that would be the bow and arrow.

That is a good way of stating the fact that a calamity could so destroy all the mutually dependent features of our technology that centuries would be required to build them up again by beginning at the bottom of the pyramid.

** **grim** 〔 grɪm 〕 *adj.* 猙獰的；可怕的　　**current** 〔'kɜ·ənt 〕 *adj.* 流行的
consist in 在於　　**remark** 〔 rɪ'mɑrk 〕 *n.* 話語
whereas 〔 hwɛr'æz 〕 *conj.* 然而；而　　**atom bomb** 原子彈
bow 〔 bo 〕 *n.* 弓（ *cf.* bow〔 baʊ 〕 *v.* 鞠躬）
arrow 〔'æro 〕 *n.* 箭　　**calamity** 〔 kə'læmətɪ 〕 *n.* 災難
mutually 〔'mjutʃʊəlɪ 〕 *adv.* 相互地　　**feature** 〔'fitʃə 〕 *n.* 特徵
technology 〔 tɛk'nɑlədʒɪ 〕 *n.* 科技　　**build up** 建立
pyramid 〔'pɪrəmɪd 〕 *n.* 金字塔

❖ Comprehension ❖

1. The author of this passage thinks the joke_____.
   - (A) is very funny
   - (B) is foolish and immature
   - (C) expresses something sad but true
   - (D) expresses a false idea

2. The author is saying that the atom bomb could _____.
   - (A) not be an effective weapon
   - (B) destroy the results of our technological development
   - (C) help us dig up ancient pyramids
   - (D) be compared to the bow and arrow

3. This passage suggests that after an atomic war, _____.
   - (A) nobody would survive
   - (B) technology would be at a low level
   - (C) there would immediately be another war
   - (D) no more wars would be fought

4. The author_____ atomic bombs.
   - (A) admires the effectiveness of
   - (B) warns against the danger of
   - (C) says we must work harder to develop
   - (D) has no clear ideas about

** *dig up* 發掘   *warn against* 警告

A Survivor

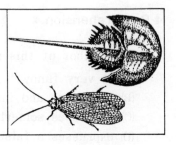

Three hundred sixty million years ago the horseshoe crab lived and looked much as it does today. It is one of the few living things that have remained unchanged since their prehistoric beginnings. The cockroach and a rare Indian Ocean fish are the only two creatures that are as old as the horseshoe crab. When the earth was still forming and mountains were rising, horseshoe crabs were already swimming in the oceans. As they are not good to eat and as they have few natural enemies, they are probably strong enough to survive for millions of years more.

** **survivor** 〔 sə'vaɪvə 〕 *n*. 生存者
horseshoe crab 大蟳蟹；鱟（＝ *king crab* ）
prehistoric 〔 ,priɪs'tɔrɪk 〕 *adj*. 史前的
cockroach 〔'kɑk,rotʃ 〕 *n*. 蟑螂　　**rare** 〔 rɛr 〕 *adj*. 稀有的
creature 〔'kritʃə 〕 *n*. 生物　　**natural enemy** 天敵
resemble 〔 rɪ'zɛmbḷ 〕 *v*. 和～相像
slightly 〔'slaɪtlɪ 〕 *adv*. 稍微
noticeably 〔'notɪsəblɪ 〕 *adv*. 明顯地　　**evolve** 〔 ɪ'vɑlv 〕 *v*. 進化

❖ Comprehension ❖

1. The main idea of this paragraph is that _____ .
   (A) horseshoe crabs lived 360 million years ago
   (B) the cockroach and a rare Indian Ocean fish are as old as the horseshoe crab
   (C) the horseshoe crab is one of the world's oldest and strongest creatures
   (D) the horseshoe crab will live for many thousands of years more

2. According to this passage, the cockroach, a certain rare Indian Ocean fish and the horseshoe crab are similar in that_____.
   (A) they swim in the oceans   (B) they are tasty
   (C) they have remained unchanged for millions of years
   (D) they resemble one another

3. From this passage, we can conclude that_____ .
   (A) horseshoe crabs first appeared just after the formation of the earth's mountains
   (B) the cockroach and a certain rare Indian Ocean fish are slightly older than the horseshoe crab
   (C) horseshoe crabs existed before the earth was fully formed
   (D) horseshoe crabs will probably exist after cockroaches have disappeared from the earth

4. _____ have noticeably changed and evolved over the past 360 million years.
   (A) Cockroaches   (B) Horseshoe crabs
   (C) Indian Ocean fish   (D) Most creatures

Dear Ann Landers

Unfair Interference

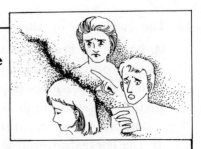

Dear Ann Landers:

I am a girl, 16. Last summer when our family went on a holiday, I met a great bunch of teenagers. No smoking, drinking. Just good, clean kids. A certain boy in the crowd (age 18) took a liking to me. We have been corresponding ever since. Last week Eddie wrote that he had saved his money and was coming to see me. He has a friend in town and had arranged to stay at his house. I was very excited and told my parents.

Yesterday Mom was acting very strange. I knew something was wrong. Finally I got it out of her. She had sent Eddie a telegram telling him to cancel his trip because I wasn't THAT interested and signed my name.

I'm very upset. Eddie was a friend, not a sweetheart. Mom says she did it for my own good because he is too old for me. I'd like your opinion.

—Unfairly Treated

Dear U.T.:

Your signature is also my opinion. Your mother should have told you of her displeasure and you should have decided together what was best.

❖ Comprehension ❖

1. The writer's mother was worried about her _____ .
    (A) smoking
    (B) drinking
    (C) grades
    (D) choice of friends

2. What did the writer's mother do about the problem?
    (A) she wrote Dear Ann Landers for help.
    (B) She sent the daughter to stay with a friend.
    (C) She started saving her money.
    (D) She sent a telegram with her daughter's name.

3. Ann Landers agreed with _____ .
    (A) the writer
    (B) the mother
    (C) Eddie
    (D) none of the above

** **interference** 〔͵ɪntɚˈfɪrəns〕 *n.* 干涉
    bunch 〔bʌntʃ〕 *n.* 群(=*group*)   ***take a liking to*** 喜歡～
    correspond 〔͵kɔrəˈspɑnd〕 *vi.* 通信
    telegram 〔ˈtɛlə͵græm〕 *n.* 電報   **cancel** 〔ˈkænsl̩〕 *v.* 取消
    upset 〔ʌpˈsɛt〕 *adj.* 難過的   **sweet-heart** 〔ˈswit͵hɑrt〕 *n.* 情人
    signature 〔ˈsɪgnətʃɚ〕 *n.* 署名
    displeasure 〔dɪsˈplɛʒɚ〕 *n.* 不高興

16 An April Fool's Trick

April 1st is a day on which, in some countries, people try to play tricks on others. If one succeeds in tricking somebody, one laughs and says, "April Fool!"

One April 1st, a country bus was going along a winding road when it slowed down and stopped. The driver turned to the passengers and said, "This poor bus is getting old. There's only one thing to do. I shall count three, and then I want you all to lean forward. That should get the bus start -ed again. Now, all of you lean back as far as you can in your seats and get ready." The passengers pressed back against their seats and waited anxiously.

"One! Two! Three!" counted the driver. The passengers all swung forward suddenly— and the bus started up at a great rate.

The passengers began to smile with relief. But their smiles turned to surprised and then delighted laughter when the driver merrily cried, "April Fool!"

** **April fool** 在愚人節（All Fools' Day）受愚弄的人

❖ Comprehension ❖

1. _____ was (were) fooled by this prank.
   (A) The driver　　　　　(B) The passengers
   (C) Both the driver and the passengers
   (D) Neither the driver nor the passengers

2. The passengers leaned forward because _____.
   (A) the bus stopped suddenly
   (B) the driver asked them to
   (C) they were on a hill
   (D) they wanted to hear the driver

3. When the bus started up again, the passengers thought that _____.
   (A) the driver might be drunk
   (B) the bus had been in an accident
   (C) the driver was too old
   (D) their action had started the bus

4. The bus had stopped because _____.
   (A) it was too old to run properly
   (B) the driver wanted to trick the passengers
   (C) the driver was drunk
   (D) the passengers had all leaned backwards

** **play tricks on** sb. 開某人的玩笑　winding〔'waɪndɪŋ〕adj. 蜿蜒的
slow down 減低速度　　**lean**〔lin〕v. 傾身
start〔start〕v. 發動(機器等)　　**press ~ against** 使~緊靠著
swung〔swʌŋ〕v. 擺動(swing 的過去式與過去分詞)
at a ~ rate 以~速度　　**prank**〔præŋk〕n. 開玩笑

17 Smoking Patterns of Teenagers

　　Teenage smoking patterns are similar in many ways to those of adults. There are fewer smokers among adolescents coming from higher socioeconomic backgrounds, and among adolescents taking college preparatory courses in high school.

　　One of the strongest influences on teenage smoking is the family's smoking habits. Adolescents are more likely to start smoking if _____ . The chances are greater that an adolescent will smoke if one or both parents do not live at home.

** **pattern**〔'pætən〕 *n.* 型式　　*be similar to* 和～類似
　　adult〔ə'dʌlt〕 *n.* 成人　　**adolescent**〔,ædḷ'ɛsənt〕 *n.* 青少年
　　socioeconomic〔,soʃɪə,ikə'namɪk〕 *adj.* 社會經濟的
　　background〔'bæk,graʊnd〕 *n.* 背景
　　preparatory〔prɪ'pærə,torɪ〕 *adj.* 預備的
　　chance〔tʃæns〕 *n.* 〔常用 *pl.*〕可能性
　　subject〔'sʌbdʒɪkt〕 *n.* 學科　　**sociology**〔,soʃɪ'alədʒɪ〕 *n.* 社會學
　　psychology〔saɪ'kalədʒɪ〕 *n.* 心理學
　　relatively〔'rɛlətɪvlɪ〕 *adv.* 比較上；相對地

❖ Comprehension ❖

1. " Socioeconomic " conditions are related with what subjects?

   (A) engineering and physics
   (B) politics and law
   (C) sociology and economics
   (D) psychology and medicine

2. Which of the following fits in the blank ?

   (A) they do not know about the medical dangers
   (B) one or both of their parents or an elder brother or sister smokes
   (C) they fail in their studies or in their social lives
   (D) they spend most of their time watching television

3. _____ among adolescents from relatively wealthy families.

   (A) Smoking is extremely rare
   (B) There are relatively fewer smokers
   (C) Family habits are not very important
   (D) Smoking patterns have not been studied

4. Adolescents _____ are more likely to become smokers.

   (A) who are taking college preparatory courses
   (B) whose parents smoke
   (C) living with both parents
   (D) from the higher social classes

18 Economy — Not Always the Best Policy

To stay within our tight budget, I asked my wife to cut my hair. She agreed but reminded me that she had no _____ . After an hour under her scissors, I emerged with my hair looking like a thatched roof.

Still bent on economizing, I presented myself at the local barber college to see if some improvement could be made. When I sat down in the chair, the student barber suddenly excused himself and returned shortly with his instructor. "He came in this way," the student was saying. "Honest! I haven't touched him."

** **economy** 〔ɪˋkɑnəmɪ〕 *n.* 節儉　　　**policy** 〔ˋpɑləsɪ〕 *n.* 策略
budget 〔ˋbʌdʒɪt〕 *n.* 預算　　　**scissors** 〔ˋsɪzəz〕 *n.pl.* 剪刀
emerge 〔ɪˋmɝdʒ〕 *vi.* 出現　　　**thatched roof** 茅草屋頂
(*be*) *bent on* 一心一意要～
economize 〔ɪˋkɑnə͵maɪz〕 *v.* 節約　　　*present oneself* 出現
improvement 〔ɪmˋpruvmənt〕 *n.* 改善
excuse oneself 請求准許離開　　　**shortly** 〔ˋʃɔrtlɪ〕 *adv.* 不久
instructor 〔ɪnˋstrʌktə〕 *n.* 教師

◈ Comprehension ◈

1. The narrator was trying to_____.
    (A) play a trick on his wife
    (B) get an excellent haircut
    (C) save money
    (D) become a skilled barber

2. Which of the following fits in the blank？
    (A) time
    (B) professional training
    (C) interest in the budget
    (D) money

3. The student barber thought that_____.
    (A) the man did not have much money
    (B) the man's hair had been badly cut
    (C) haircutting was a poor profession
    (D) the narrator's wife was skillful

4. The student barber was afraid that_____.
    (A) he would make a mistake in cutting the man's hair
    (B) the narrator would become angry at him
    (C) his teacher would blame him for the man's haircut
    (D) the man would not pay him enough money

** **narrator**〔næ'retɚ〕 *n.* 敘述者
professional〔prə'fɛʃənḷ〕*n.* 專業的

19 A Practical Student

There is the story of the little boy in Kentucky who was asked a test question : " If you went to a store and bought six cents worth of candy and gave the clerk ten cents, what change would you receive ? " The boy replied: " I never had ten cents and if I had I wouldn't spend it on candy and anyway candy is what mother makes." The tester reformulated the question : " If you had taken ten cows to pasture for your father and six of them strayed away, how many ____ⓐ____ to drive home ? " The boy replied : "We don't have ten cows, but if we ____ⓑ____ and I ____ⓒ____ six I wouldn't dare go home. " Undeterred, the tester pressed his question : " If there were ten children in your school and six of them were sick with the measles, how many would there be in school ? " The answer came : "None, because the rest would be afraid of catching it too. "

** **change** 〔 tʃendʒ 〕 *n*. 找錢
   tester〔'tɛstɚ〕 *n*. 主試者(*cf*. testee 受試者)

◆ Comprehension ◆

1. The tester was trying to test the boy's_____.
   (A) understanding of a mathematical concept
   (B) honesty and obedience to parents and teachers
   (C) ability to understand complex language
   (D) maturity and general character

2. What should go in the blank marked ⓐ?
   (A) should you leave (B) had you left
   (C) have you left (D) would you have left

3. What should go in the blanks marked ⓑ and ⓒ ?
   (A) did − lost (B) do −lose
   (C) have got − have lost (D) shall do − shall lose

4. In answering the tester's questions, the boy_____.
   (A) made mathematical mistakes
   (B) interpreted the examples too literally
   (C) showed that he was dishonest and disobedient
   (D) made the tester angry and impatient

** **reformulate**〔ri'fɔrmjə,let〕 *vt.* 再形成
  pasture〔'pæstʃə〕 *n.* 牧場 **stray**〔stre〕 *v.* 走失
  undeterred〔,ʌndı'tɝd〕 *adj.* 未受阻的 **press**〔prɛs〕 *v.* 堅持
  measles〔'miz̩z〕 *n.* 麻疹 **concept**〔'kɑnsɛpt〕 *n.* 概念
  obedience〔ə'bidı əns〕 *n.* 順從 **interpret**〔ın'tɝprıt〕 *v.* 解釋
  literally〔'lıtərəlı〕 *adv.* 照字面地（ *cf.* literary 文學的）

20 A Hesitant General

During the period of the Civil War, Abraham Lincoln's problems were very great. The North had no trained army. It had no good general. During the first year or two of the war, the North changed the commander-in-chief of its army several times. One of these early generals was General George McClellan.

McClellan was a good general, but he was a very careful man. It seems that he was too careful to be a first-rate general. He always waited and waited, prepared and prepared before making an attack. Everybody, including Lincoln, _____ patience with him. Lincoln wrote him a letter. He said:

"My dear McClellan : If you don't want to use the army, I should like to borrow it for a while.

Yours respectfully,

A. Lincoln"

** **hesitant**〔ˈhɛzətənt〕*adj.* 猶豫不決的　　**general**〔ˈdʒɛnərəl〕*n.* 將軍
　　the Civil War 美國南北戰爭(1861 — 1865)

◈ Comprehension ◈

1. In the first year or two of the American Civil War, _____ .

   (A) the North had a well-trained army, but poor generals
   (B) there were several different commanders of the Northern army
   (C) George McClellan was the only leader of the Northern army
   (D) Abraham Lincoln was satisfied with the performance of his generals

2. Lincoln thought that General McClellan was _____ .

   (A) not a loyal soldier (B) being too cautious
   (C) a first-rate general (D) killed in a battle

3. What word fits in the blank?

   (A) added (B) blamed
   (C) lost (D) got

4. From the letter, we see that Lincoln _____ McClellan.

   (A) was pleased with (B) was frustrated with
   (C) hated (D) loved

** **commander-in-chief** 總司令 **first-rate** 〔'fɝst'ret〕 *adj.* 第一流的
   Yours respectfully 〔 *Respectfully yours* 〕敬上（信尾敬語）
   performance 〔pɚ'fɔrməns〕 *n.* 表現
   cautious 〔'kɔʃəs〕 *adj.* 謹慎的
   be frustrated with 對～失望

21

A Wise Grandmother

Stopping by my mother's house for a visit, I discovered that my older brother and two of his children were also there. Jim's boys, aged seven and nine, were soon running about the house, slamming doors and making a general nuisance of themselves.

When their racket making had reached a peak, Jim reprimanded them quite harshly. Mother, however, quickly came to the boys' defense, telling Jim not to be so hard on them. "Mother!" snapped Jim. "They are my children, and I have the perfect right to correct them."

Mother smiled and said softly, "I am glad that we agree, Jim. I was correcting mine."

** **stop by** 中途作短暫訪問　　**slam**〔slæm〕 *v.* 用力關

make a nuisance of oneself 惹人討厭

make a racket 大聲喧嘩　　**peak**〔pik〕 *n.* 頂點

reprimand〔͵rɛprə'mænd〕 *v.* 譴責

harshly〔'harʃlɪ〕 *adv.* 嚴厲地　　**come to** *one's* **defense** 護著某人

❖ Comprehension ❖

1. Jim is_____.
    (A) the narrator of this story
    (B) one of the narrator's sons
    (C) the narrator's brother
    (D) slamming doors

2. "Racket"means the same as _____ .
    (A) noise
    (B) reprimands
    (C) play
    (D) correcting

3. The narrator's mother told Jim_____.
    (A) not to scold his children so harshly
    (B) that his children were a nuisance
    (C) to stop slamming doors
    (D) to make his children behave better

4. Jim insisted that_____ .
    (A) his children were not making a nuisance
    (B) it was his right to slam doors
    (C) his mother should not scold his children harshly
    (D) he had a right to scold his children

** *be hard on* 對～嚴厲   **snap**〔snæp〕*v.* 吼著說
    scold〔skold〕*v.* 責罵

Valuable Salt

Most of us use salt every day. We use it to make our food taste better. We think nothing of it. It is there, and we use it. There was a time, however, when salt was not so common.

In the ancient world, salt was a luxury and only for the rich. Greek tales tell of people who did not live near the sea. They used no salt in their food. Salt was once so hard to get that it was used as money. Roman workers were once paid all or part of their wages in salt. That is why we have the expression "not worth his salt." The English word "salary" comes from the Latin word, *salarium*, which means "salt money."

** **valuable** 〔'væljʊəb!〕 *adj.* 貴重的　**ancient** 〔'enʃənt〕 *adj.* 古代的
　luxury 〔'lʌkʃərɪ〕 *n.* 奢侈品　　**wage** 〔wedʒ〕 *n.* 工資
　not worth one's salt 不能稱職　　**salary** 〔'sælərɪ〕 *n.* 薪水
　take ~ for granted 視~爲理所當然

❖ Comprehension ❖

1. Although people now take salt for granted, it used to be_____ .
   (A) completely unknown
   (B) a valuable luxury
   (C) illegally used
   (D) only used in Greece

2. In the ancient world, only_____used salt.
   (A) rich people
   (B) people who lived near the sea
   (C) Roman workers
   (D) salaried employees

3. The passage implies that ancient peoples obtained salt mostly from_____.
   (A) Rome
   (B) mines
   (C) the sea
   (D) Greece

4. The author explains the origin of the word " salary " to show_____.
   (A) how quickly languages change
   (B) how close English is to Latin
   (C) that we no longer value salt
   (D) that salt used to be used as money

** **illegally** 〔ɪˊlɪglɪ〕 *adv*. 不合法地   **obtain** 〔əbˊten〕 *v*. 獲得
mine 〔maɪn〕 *n*. 礦山

Alienation and Aging

As one grows older, one becomes more silent.

In one's youth one is ready to pour oneself out to the world; one feels an intense fellowship with other people, one wants to throw oneself in their arms and one feels that they will receive one; one wants to open oneself to them so that they may take one, one wants to penetrate into them; one's life seems to overflow into the lives of others and become one with others as the waters become one in the sea.

But gradually the power one felt of doing all this leaves one; a barrier rises up between oneself and one's fellows, and one realizes that they are strangers to one.

————— *W. S. Maugham*

** **alienation** 〔͵eljə′neʃən〕 *n*. 疏遠   ***pour out*** 傾吐
   intense 〔ɪn′tɛns〕 *adj*. 深切的   **fellowship** 〔′fɛlo͵ʃɪp〕 *n*. 友誼
   penetrate 〔′pɛnə͵tret〕 *v*. 滲入   **overflow** 〔͵ovə′flo〕 *v*. 溢出來
   barrier 〔′bærɪə〕 *n*. 壁壘
   Maugham 〔mɔm〕 *n*. 毛姆 (英國作家)

❖ Comprehension ❖

1. As a person becomes older, he becomes more_____.
   - (A) silent
   - (B) powerful
   - (C) intense
   - (D) open

2. According to the above passage, one has a strong interest in others when _____.
   - (A) one is young
   - (B) one is old
   - (C) one is healthy
   - (D) something blocks their friendship

3. Young people tend to do all of the following EXCEPT _____.
   - (A) throw themselves into others' arms
   - (B) feel fellowship with others
   - (C) pour themselves out into the world
   - (D) throw up barriers

4. The line, " the waters become one in the sea," refers to_____.
   - (A) death
   - (B) wisdom
   - (C) fellowship
   - (D) travel

** **block** 〔blɑk〕 *v*. 妨礙   ***throw up*** 趕造

24 A Terrifying Moment

Dick found it necessary to get two jobs at the same time so as to earn enough money to pay for his education.

One summer he managed to get a job in a butcher's shop during the daytime, and another in a hospital at night. In the shop, the butcher often left him to do all the serving while he went into another room to do the accounts. In the hospital, on the other hand, he was, of course, allowed to do only the simplest jobs, like helping to carry people from one part of the hospital to another. Both at the butcher's shop and at the hospital, Dick had to wear white clothes.

One evening at the hospital, Dick had to help to carry a woman from her bed to the place where she was to have an operation. The woman was already feeling frightened, but when she saw Dick, that finished her. " No! No! " she cried. " Not my butcher! _____ "and fainted away.

** ***manage to*** 設法 butcher〔'bʊtʃɚ〕 *n.* 肉商;屠夫
butcher's(**shop**)肉店 account〔ə'kaʊnt〕*n.* 帳

❖ Comprehension ❖

1. Dick had two jobs because _____ .
   (A) he had too much free time
   (B) the experience was valuable
   (C) he needed the money
   (D) he liked white clothes

2. Which one fits in the blank?
   (A) I'm so happy to see somebody familiar !
   (B) Why aren't you at the butcher's shop today?
   (C) I won't be operated on by my butcher !
   (D) Isn't your name Dick?

3. In the hospital, Dick _____ .
   (A) only did simple jobs
   (B) earned a lot of money
   (C) did the accounts
   (D) operated on a woman

4. The woman in the hospital was _____ .
   (A) happy to recognize somebody familiar
   (B) very poor
   (C) wearing white clothes
   (D) a customer of Dick's butcher's shop

** operation 〔͵ɑpə'reʃən〕 n. 手術   frightened 〔'fraɪtənd〕 adj. 害怕的
   finish 〔'fɪnɪʃ〕 v. 〔口〕殺死；毀滅
   faint 〔fent〕 vi. 暈倒   operate on 為～動手術

Not That Kind of Painter!

The struggling young artist and his wife were at a party, and one of the guests asked the man what he did for a living. "I'm a painter," he replied.

"That's great!" answered the guest. "The walls in my house could use a new coat of paint. I'll give you nine hundred dollars to do the job."

"But you don't understand," said the artist. "I'm a painter. You know, like Michelangelo."

"What does that mean?" asked the guest.

The artist's wife chimed in, "You said nine hundred dollars?"

"That's right," was the reply.

"It means," she responded, "that he'd be happy to paint your ceiling as well."

** **struggling** 〔'strʌglɪŋ〕*adj.* 必須努力掙扎才能謀生的
　　could use〔美俗〕需要（＝*need*）
　　coat〔kot〕*n.* 在外表上所塗的一層

◈ Comprehension ◈

1. This story is about _____ .
    (A) a famous painter
    (B) a well-known artist
    (C) a man who paints houses for a living
    (D) an artist who is not very successful

2. The guest at the party thinks the man is _____ .
    (A) Michelangelo
    (B) telling a lie
    (C) a house-painter
    (D) a talented artist

3. The painter thinks that the guest's offer is _____ .
    (A) unrelated to his profession
    (B) too much money
    (C) not enough money
    (D) a joke or perhaps a trick

4. The man's wife is clearly _____ .
    (A) offended by the guest's offer
    (B) in love with her husband
    (C) ashamed of her husband
    (D) concerned about money

** **Michelangelo** 〔͵mɪklʲˈændʒəˌlo〕*n.* 米開蘭基羅（義大利畫家、雕刻家、
建築家、詩人）
　　chime in 插嘴　　**respond** 〔rɪˈspɑnd〕*v.* 回答
　　ceiling 〔ˈsilɪŋ〕*n.* 天花板　　***as well*** 也；亦
　　offer 〔ˈɔfɚ〕*n.* 建議　　***be concerned about*** 關心

26 The IRS Strikes Again

A little boy who had lost his father and whose widowed mother was having a difficult time making ends meet, wrote a letter:

" Dear God: Will you please send my mother $100 because she is having a hard time? "

The letter ended up in the General Post Office, and the employee who opened it was touched. He put a few dollars aside and collected a total of $50 among the other postal employees to whom he showed the letter, and the money was sent to the little boy. Several weeks later the little boy again wrote, this time a letter of thanks. But he also pointed out that God had made the mistake of sending the letter through Washington and that as usual, they had deducted 50 percent of the money.

** **IRS** 美國國稅局(= *Internal Revenue Service*)
widowed 〔'wɪdod〕 *adj*. 喪偶的　　*make ends meet* 使收支平衡
have a hard time 遭遇困難　　**General Post Office** 郵政總局
employee 〔,ɛmplɔɪ'i〕 *n*. 職員　　**touch** 〔tʌtʃ〕 *v*. 感動
put aside 儲蓄；存　　**total** 〔'totl〕 *n*. 總計

✦ Comprehension ✦

1. The little boy's father_____ .
   (A) had lost his job and needed money
   (B) was dead
   (C) worked for the Post Office
   (D) came from Washington

2. The postal employee who opened the letter_____ .
   (A) collected money and sent it to the boy
   (B) seemed to know the boy's father
   (C) suspected that the boy was playing a trick
   (D) took away 50% of the money they had received

3. The boy thinks that_____ .
   (A) his father is still alive and lives in Washington
   (B) God sent the money, but the U.S. government kept half of it as tax
   (C) his mother is not generous enough with him, so he needs more money
   (D) when he grows up, he will become a postal employee

4. The paragraph pokes fun at _____ .
   (A) the post office   (B) religion
   (C) the U.S. government   (D) childhood

** **postal** 〔'post!〕 *adj*. 郵局的   ***point out*** 指出
   as usual 照例   **deduct** 〔dɪ'dʌkt〕 *vt*. 扣除
   suspect 〔sə'spɛkt〕 *v*. 懷疑   ***poke fun at*** 嘲弄

㉗ Never Satisfied

A young boy and his doting grandmother were walking along the shore in Miami Beach when a huge wave appeared out of nowhere, sweeping the child out to sea. The horrified woman fell on her knees, raised her eyes to the heavens and begged the Lord to return her beloved grandson.

And, lo, another wave reared up and deposited the stunned child on the sand before her. The grandmother looked the boy over carefully. He was fine. But still she stared up angrily toward the heavens. "When we came," she snapped indignantly, "he had a hat!"

** **doting** 〔'dotɪŋ〕 *adj.* 溺愛的　　**nowhere** 〔'no,hwɛr〕 *n.* 無處
sweep 〔swip〕 *v.* 捲走；沖走　　**horrified** 〔'hɔrə,faɪd〕 *adj.* 驚駭的
heavens 〔'hɛvənz〕 *n.pl.* 天空　　**beloved** 〔bɪ'lʌvd〕 *adj.* 所愛的
lo 〔lo〕 *interj.*〔古〕看哪！　　**rear** 〔rɪr〕 *v.* 抬起
deposit 〔dɪ'pazɪt〕 *v.* 放下　　**stunned** 〔stʌnd〕 *adj.* 嚇呆的
look over 檢查　　**snap** 〔snæp〕 *v.* 聲音尖而快地說
indignantly 〔ɪn'dɪgnəntlɪ〕 *adv.* 憤慨地

❖ Comprehension ❖

1. What were the boy and his grandmother doing?
   - (A) swimming
   - (B) praying
   - (C) walking
   - (D) arguing

2. A doting grandmother _____ her grandchild.
   - (A) scolds
   - (B) loves
   - (C) babysits
   - (D) spanks

3. Why was the woman horrified?
   - (A) Because she fell on her knees.
   - (B) Because her hat got wet.
   - (C) Because the child was stunned.
   - (D) Because the child was gone.

4. How did the woman react when God answered her prayer?
   - (A) She was grateful.
   - (B) She was angry.
   - (C) She changed her mind.
   - (D) She was stunned.

** **scold** 〔skold〕 *v*. 叱責   **spank** 〔spæŋk〕 *v*. 打
   prayer 〔prɛr〕 *n*. 祈禱   **grateful** 〔'gretfəl〕 *adj*. 感激的

A Playboy

Across the street from us lives a retired man who often sits on his porch to watch the doings of his neighbors. I am a teacher by day, and I dress conservatively. In my spare time, however, I am active in the theater, and come and go in a variety of costumes and wigs.

One afternoon my husband was putting out the garbage when our neighbor approached him. " How do you manage to bring all those women in and out of there without your wife finding out? " he inquired.

My husband just laughed and winked. Later, when I heard the story, I asked, " You did tell him the truth? "

" What ! " my husband exclaimed, " And ruin my reputation? "

** **porch**〔portʃ〕 *n*. 走廊　**conservatively**〔kən'sɝvɪtɪvlɪ〕 *adv*.保守地
　　spare time 閒暇　　　*be active in* 積極參與~
　　costume〔'kɑstjum〕 *n*. 服裝　　**wig**〔wɪg〕 *n*. 假髮
　　put out 拿出去丟　　**approach**〔ə'protʃ〕 *v*. 走近
　　manage to 設法做；達成　　**wink**〔wɪŋk〕 *v*. 眨眼

✦ Comprehension ✦

1. The writer of this story is_____.

   (A) married to a teacher
   (B) a retired actor
   (C) intimately involved with many women
   (D) a teacher whose hobby is acting

2. The neighbor thinks that_____.

   (A) many different women visit the writer's house
   (B) the teacher is also retired
   (C) acting is not a respectable profession
   (D) women should always dress conservatively

3. The husband wants to maintain his reputation as
   _____.

   (A) a playboy who enjoys the love of many girls
   (B) a conservative, respectable teacher
   (C) an ordinary, retired person
   (D) a successful and talented actor

4. The reader is led to believe that the _____ is rather
   nosy.

   (A) actress   (B) husband
   (C) teacher   (D) neighbor

** **exclaim** 〔ɪk'sklem〕 *v.* 大叫   **ruin** 〔'ruɪn〕 *v.* 毀掉
   reputation 〔,rɛpjə'teʃən〕 *n.* 名譽
   intimately 〔'ɪntəmɪtlɪ〕 *adv.* 親密地   *be involved with*～ 和～有瓜葛
   maintain 〔men'ten〕 *v.* 保持   **nosy** 〔'nozɪ〕 *adj.* 好管閒事的

A Man of Principle

Our crew set about catching cod, and hauled up a great many. Hitherto I had stuck to my resolution of not eating animal food, and on this occasion I considered, with my master Tryon, the taking of every fish as a kind of unprovoked murder, since none of them had done, or ever could do us any injury that might justify the slaughter. All this seemed very reasonable. But I had formerly been a great lover of fish, and, when this came hot out of the frying-pan, it smelled admirably well. I balanced some time between principle and inclination, till I recollected that, when the fish were opened, I saw smaller fish taken out of their stomachs; then thought I, " If you eat one another, I don't see why we mayn't eat you." So I dined upon cod very heartily.

"The Autobiography of Benjamin Franklin"

** *set about* 開始　　**cod**〔kɑd〕*n.* 鱈魚
haul〔hɔl〕*v.* 拖；拉　　**hitherto**〔,hɪðɚ'tu〕*adv.* 迄今
stick to 堅守　　**unprovoked**〔,ʌnprə'vokt〕*adj.* 無正當理由的
justify〔'dʒʌstə,faɪ〕*v.* 證明～爲正當

✦ Comprehension ✦

1. When the author smelled the fish cooking, _____.
   (A) he felt like eating some
   (B) he decided not to eat any
   (C) he felt pity for it
   (D) he became very sick

2. " Stuck to my resolution" means_____.
   (A) made an important decision
   (B) changed a decision I had made
   (C) kept to a decision I had made
   (D) refused to make a decision

3. Franklin decided that he would eat some fish because _____.
   (A) the other crew members were eating some
   (B) his master, Tryon, liked to eat fish
   (C) he remembered that big fish ate small fish
   (D) there was no other food for him to eat

4. Franklin is describing how he stopped being a _____.
   (A) fisherman   (B) meat-eater
   (C) vegetarian   (D) thinker

** slaughter〔'slɔtɚ〕 n. 屠殺   admirably〔'ædmərəblɪ〕adv. 極佳地
balance 〔'bæləns〕v. 猶豫不決   inclination〔,ɪnklə'neʃən〕n.愛好
recollect〔,rɛkə'lɛkt〕v. 想起   dine upon 以～爲食
heartily〔'hɑrtɪlɪ〕adv. 痛快地   keep to 嚴守
vegetarian〔,vɛdʒə'tɛrɪən〕n. 素食者

30 The Vital Role of Risk

Risk is an essential need of the soul. The absence of risk produces a type of boredom which paralyzes in a different way from fear, but almost as much. Risk is a form of danger which provokes a rational reaction; that is to say, it doesn't go beyond the soul's resources to the point of crushing the soul beneath a load of fear.

The protection of mankind from fear and terror doesn't imply the abolition of risk; it implies, on the contrary, the permanent presence of a certain amount of risk in all aspects of social life; for the absence of risk weakens courage to the point of *leaving the soul, if the need should arise, without the slightest inner protection against fear.* All that is wanted is for risk to offer itself under such conditions that it is not transformed into a sensation of fatality.

** **essential** 〔ə'sɛnʃəl〕 *adj*. 必要的　　**boredom** 〔'bɔrdəm〕 *n*. 厭倦
　paralyze 〔'pærə,laɪz〕 *v*. 使麻痺　　**provoke** 〔prə'vok〕 *v*. 引起
　rational 〔'ræʃənl〕 *adj*. 理性的　　**reaction** 〔rɪ'ækʃən〕 *n*. 反應
　resource 〔rɪ'sors, 'risors〕 *n*. 方法；手段

❖ Comprehension ❖

1. Risk is a form of _____ .
   (A) fear   (B) reaction
   (C) danger   (D) fatality

2. The "abolition of risk" would mean _____ .
   (A) more risk
   (B) no more risk
   (C) permanent risk
   (D) dangerous risk

3. Boredom paralyzes people _____ fear.
   (A) more than
   (B) less than
   (C) the same as
   (D) who feel

4. According to this passage, people who do not experience risks _____ .
   (A) are unlikely to have serious accidents
   (B) lack courage and are unable to deal with fear
   (C) provoke other people to take rational actions
   (D) tend to live longer than people who take risks

** **crush** 〔krʌʃ〕 v. 崩潰；粉碎   **imply** 〔ɪmˈplaɪ〕 v. 表示
abolition 〔͵æbəˈlɪʃən〕 n. 廢除   **permanent** 〔ˈpɝmənənt〕 adj.永久的
need 〔nid〕 n. 急難   **arise** 〔əˈraɪz〕 v. 發生
transform 〔trænsˈfɔrm〕 v. 改變   **sensation** 〔sɛnˈseʃən〕 n. 感覺
fatality 〔fəˈtælətɪ〕 n. 致命

Dear Abby

Gratitude

Dear Abby :

Many years ago, my aunt trudged through the wind and snow one morning to her rural mailbox. Upon opening it, she found a little black and white mongrel pup — sick and nearly frozen stiff. She took the little guy into her home, named him Tony, and nursed him back to health. Everyone thought she was crazy.

Twenty years later, on another cold, snowy winter night, old Tony, arthritic and hard of hearing, roused my aunt from a second-story bedroom and guided her to safety while her house burned down around them.

When the firemen finally arrived, all that remained was the fireplace with its two-story chimney, Tony and my aunt!

How's that for gratitude? — Marion, Las Vegas.

Dear Marion :

Beautiful! And it will please you and other readers to learn that according to my most recent reader mail, the numbers have shifted dramatically in favor of attempting to nurse the dogs back to health as opposed to putting them out of their misery with a shotgun.

❖ Comprehension ❖

1. What did Marion's aunt find in her mailbox?
   (A) a letter from Marion
   (B) a letter to Dear Abby
   (C) a dog
   (D) a package

2. Which of the following was destroyed by the fire?
   (A) the fireplace   (B) the chimney
   (C) the bedroom   (D) Tony

3. How did Tony show his gratitude?
   (A) By nursing Marion back to health.
   (B) By learning to fetch the mail.
   (C) By saving the life of Marion's aunt.
   (D) By burning the house down.

** **gratitude** 〔'grætə‚tjud〕 *n.* 感恩   **trudge** 〔trʌdʒ〕 *vi.* 吃力地走
rural 〔'rʊrəl〕 *adj.* 田園的；鄉下的
mongrel 〔'mʌŋgrəl〕 *adj.* 雜種的
pup 〔pʌp〕 *n.* 小狗   **stiff** 〔stɪf〕 *adj.* 僵硬的
arthritic 〔ɑr'θrɪtɪk〕 *adj.* 關節炎的
hard of hearing 重聽的   **rouse** 〔raʊz〕 *v.* 叫醒
burn down 燒毀   **fireplace** 〔'faɪr‚ples〕 *n.* 壁爐
shift 〔ʃɪft〕 *v.* 改變   **dramatically** 〔drə'mætɪkəlɪ〕 *adv.* 戲劇性地
in favor of 贊成   ***as opposed to*** 與～相對的
misery 〔'mɪzərɪ〕 *n.* 痛苦
fetch 〔fɛtʃ〕 *v.* 取來

③1 Deciphering Faces

It is not that I judge people by their appearance, but it is true that I am fascinated by their faces. I do not stare in their presence. I like to take the impression of a face home with me, there to stare at and chew over it in privacy, as a wild beast prefers to devour its prey in concealment.

As a means of judging character it is a misleading practice. The misleading element, in fact, provides the essence of my satisfaction. In the course of deciphering a face, its shape, tones, and lines, as if these were words and sentences of a message from the interior, I fix upon it a character which, though I know it to be distorted, never quite untrue, never entirely true, interests me. I am as near the mark as myth is to history. I seek no justification for this habit, but it is one of the things I do.

** **decipher** 〔dɪˈsaɪfɚ〕 *vt.* 辨讀　　**fascinate** 〔ˈfæsn̩ˌet〕 *v.* 使著迷
impression 〔ɪmˈprɛʃən〕 *n.* 印象　　**chew** 〔tʃu〕 *v.* 玩味；深思
in privacy 私底下　　**devour** 〔dɪˈvaʊr〕 *vt.* 吞食
prey 〔pre〕 *n.* 被捕食的動物　　**concealment** 〔kənˈsilmənt〕 *n.* 隱蔽的場所
misleading 〔mɪsˈlidɪŋ〕 *adj.* 產生誤解的　　**essence** 〔ˈɛsn̩s〕 *n.* 要素；主因

✦ Comprehension ✦

1. The writer of this passage_____.
   (A) hates people who stare at others
   (B) stares at people when he sees them
   (C) is very interested in faces
   (D) is very proud of his face

2. In this passage, the author_____ habit.
   (A) says he is ashamed of his
   (B) describes and explains his
   (C) complains about an annoying
   (D) attempts to justify a

3. According to the author, judging a person's character
   from his face is_____.
   (A) a very bad habit because the character is misunderstood
   (B) generally fairly accurate and therefore useful
   (C) not accurate, but nonetheless interesting
   (D) the cause of many serious misunderstandings

4. The author thinks that myth and history_____.
   (A) are the best justification for his habit
   (B) are really the same thing
   (C) aren't exactly alike, but aren't entirely different
   (D) are useful in helping us understand a man's character

** **interior** 〔ɪn'tɪrɪɚ〕 *n.* 內部   *fix upon* 把～歸給
   distort 〔dɪs'tɔrt〕 *v.* 扭曲   **myth** 〔mɪθ〕 *n.* 杜撰的故事
   justification 〔‚dʒʌstəfə'keʃən〕 *n.* 辯白

32 Sex Discrimination

SAN DIEGO (UPI)—All five women trainees for the fire department flunked out, four because they were not strong enough and one for getting hurt.

" Strength is the main problem," said Fire Chief Leonard Bell after the five women were dismissed from the Fire Academy Tuesday.

" We don't say women can't do the job. We just say these women didn't have the strength to do the job," he said.

The women meanwhile called a news conference to say they might hire an attorney to sue the city for sex discrimination, and were seeking support from women's rights groups.

" The training was directly geared at phasing out all the women," complained Carol Tyler, 26, a former lifeguard.

** **discrimination** 〔dɪ‚skrɪmə'neʃən〕 *n.* 歧視
UPI 合衆國際社(= *United Press International*)
trainee 〔tren'i〕 *n.* 受訓練的人　**flunk out** (成績不良而)退學；退訓
dismiss 〔dɪs'mɪs〕 *v.* 開除　　**academy** 〔ə'kædəmɪ〕 *n.* 學院

❖ Comprehension ❖

1. The fire chief said that these women_____.
   - (A) were too weak to be firemen
   - (B) weren't intelligent enough
   - (C) didn't deserve to have a job
   - (D) didn't study hard enough

2. This passage implies that in San Diego_____.
   - (A) men and women are treated equally
   - (B) women are treated better than men
   - (C) men are treated better than women
   - (D) women should stay at home and not work

3. The women were considering hiring a(n)_____.
   - (A) lifeguard　　　　　(B) fireman
   - (C) attorney　　　　　(D) newscaster

4. Carol Tyler said that the training was_____.
   - (A) direct and good for women
   - (B) bad for women
   - (C) unfair to women
   - (D) fair to women

＊＊ meanwhile 〔'min,hwaɪl〕*adv*. 在此時
　　news conference 記者招待會　　**attorney** 〔ə'tɜnɪ〕*n*. 律師
　　sue 〔su〕*v*. 控告　　**gear** 〔gɪr〕*v*. 使配合
　　phase out 逐漸淘汰　　**lifeguard** 〔'laɪf,gɑrd〕*n*. 救生員
　　deserve 〔dɪ'zɜv〕*v*. 應得
　　newscaster 〔'njuz,kæstɚ〕*n*. 新聞播報員

33 Transmission of Culture

As the child grows up, surrounded by brothers and sisters, his parents and sometimes by a member of the extended family group, he gradually learns things about the society in which he lives. In other words, the child will learn the culture of his society through his contact with, at first, the members of his family. The way in which an individual acquires the culture of his society is known as "socialization". Socialization is not confined _____ communication and the relationship between parents and their children, nor does it finish in childhood but it goes on throughout life. At the present time, research by social scientists indicates that the early years of socialization are important in the development of the individual because they have lasting effects on his ideas and attitudes.

** **transmission** 〔træns'mɪʃən〕 n. 傳播　**surround** 〔sə'raʊnd〕 v. 包圍
extended family 大家庭　　*in other words* 換句話說
contact 〔'kɑntækt〕 n. 接觸　　**individual** 〔,ɪndə'vɪdʒʊəl〕 n. 個人
acquire 〔ə'kwaɪr〕 v. 獲得；學得
socialization 〔,soʃələ'zeʃən〕 n. 社會化　**confine** 〔kən'faɪn〕 v. 限制

❖ Comprehension ❖

1. Which of the following means the same as the phrase
   " in other words ? "
   (A) that is to say   (B) on the other hand
   (C) in contrast   (D) in addition

2. What word fits in the blank?
   (A) with   (B) to
   (C) of   (D) upon

3. Which is true according to the passage ?
   (A) The child will acquire his culture only through contact
   with his family members.
   (B) Researchers report that the early years of socialization are not very important.
   (C) The child's socialization is directly related to his
   society rather than to his parents.
   (D) Socialization means that an individual acquires the
   culture of his society through both his family and
   other people.

4. The early years of a person's life have lasting effects
   on his_____.
   (A) society   (B) family
   (C) culture   (D) ideas and attitudes

** **research** 〔'rɪsɝtʃ,rɪ'sɝtʃ〕 *n.* 研究
   indicate 〔'ɪndə,ket〕 *v.* 指出   ***have effects on*** 對～有影響

The Greatest Regret

I doubt if there is anything in my life that I regret more bitterly than I do my frequent failure as a boy to bring delight to my parents by showing them how pleased I was.

Time after time, I realize now, I must have brought them bewilderment, dismay, and aching disappointment, by failing to respond adequately to some treat they planned for me. When, for example, they took me to London and to the Franco-British Exhibition, what a misery I must have been! There has always been in me a little devil that will not allow me to show pleasure when it is expected of me.

** **regret** 〔rɪ'grɛt〕 *n., vt.* 懊悔　　**bitterly** 〔'bɪtəlɪ〕 *adv.* 悲痛地
bewilderment 〔bɪ'wɪldəmənt〕 *n.* 困惑
dismay 〔dɪs'me〕 *n.* 沮喪　　**aching** 〔'ekɪŋ〕 *adj.* 心痛的
respond to　對～有反應　　**adequately** 〔'ædəkwɪtlɪ〕 *adv.* 適當地
treat 〔trit〕 *n.* 極佳的事物　　**Franco-** 〔'fræŋko〕 *pref.* (字首)法國的
exhibition 〔͵ɛksə'bɪʃən〕 *n.* 博覽會
misery 〔'mɪzərɪ〕 *n.* 痛苦　　*expect A of B*　期待A做B

◈ Comprehension ◈

1. When the author's parents took him to London_____.
   (A) he told them he was unhappy
   (B) he didn't know his parents were unhappy
   (C) he didn't show pleasure
   (D) he wanted to go home

2. The author thinks he was_____when he was a boy.
   (A) useless
   (B) helpful
   (C) polite
   (D) unappreciative

3. Which statement is the main idea of the passage?
   (A) Children should tell their parents when they are happy.
   (B) Parents should not make their children unhappy.
   (C) Children should not make their parents unhappy.
   (D) Parents should tell their children when they are happy.

4. What does "it" in the last sentence refer to?
   (A) the devil
   (B) misery
   (C) to show pleasure
   (D) the Franco-British Exhibition

** **unappreciative** 〔ˌʌnəˈprɪʃɪˌetɪv〕 *adj*. 不知感恩的

Emotions:
Express,
Don't Repress

If a child is punished for showing anger, or shamed too much for showing fear, or perhaps made fun of for showing love, he learns that expressing his real feelings is "wrong."

Some children learn that it is sinful or wrong only to express the "bad emotions" — anger and fear. But when you inhibit bad emotions, you also inhibit the expression of good emotions. And the yardstick for judging emotions is not "goodness" or "badness," as such, but appropriateness and inappropriateness. It is appropriate for the man who meets with the bear on the trail to experience fear. It is appropriate to experience anger if there is a legitimate need to destroy an obstacle by sheer force and destructiveness. Properly directed and controlled, anger is an important element of courage.

** **express** 〔ɪk'sprɛs〕 *v*. 表達　　**repress** 〔rɪ'prɛs〕 *v*. 抑制
sinful 〔'sɪnfəl〕 *adj*. 有罪的　　**inhibit** 〔ɪn'hɪbɪt〕 *v*. 抑制
yardstick 〔'jɑrd,stɪk〕 *n*. 評判或比較的標準

❖ Comprehension ❖

1. The author seems to feel that children _____.

   (A) are often punished too cruelly
   (B) should be taught to keep their emotions under control
   (C) often learn that it is wrong to express their emotions
   (D) should not be put into dangerous situations

2. The author feels that emotions should be judged on their
   _____.

   (A) effectiveness   (B) goodness
   (C) appropriateness   (D) need

3. Anger can be an important part of _____.

   (A) fear   (B) love
   (C) badness   (D) courage

4. The main topic of this paragraph is _____.

   (A) the difference between good and bad emotions
   (B) about teaching children to control their emotions
   (C) about expressing appropriate emotions
   (D) self-control

** *as such* 本身   **appropriateness** 〔ə'proprɪɪtnɪs〕 *n.* 適當
   trail 〔trel〕 *n.* 小徑   **legitimate** 〔lɪ'dʒɪtəmɪt〕 *adj.* 合理的
   sheer 〔ʃɪr〕 *adj.* 純粹的   **destructiveness** 〔dɪ'strʌktɪvnɪs〕 *n.* 破壞性
   effectiveness 〔ɪ'fɛktɪvnɪs〕 *n.* 有效性
   self-control 〔,sɛlfkən'trol〕 *n.* 自制

36 Outwitted

" You will have exactly two hours, " said the professor as he handed out examination papers to a roomful of students. " Under no circumstances will I accept a paper given to me after the deadline has passed. " Two hours later he broke the silence. " Time is up, " he said. But one student continued to work furiously.

The professor was glaring out from behind the pile of exams when the tardy student approached him, almost 15 minutes later, with his exam clutched behind his back. When the professor refused to accept it, the student drew himself up to full stature and asked, " Professor, do you know who I am ? "

" No, " said the professor.

" Terrific, " replied the student, and he stuffed his paper into the middle of the pile.

** **outwit**〔aʊt'wɪt〕vt. 以機智勝過   **hand out** 分發
roomful〔'rum,fʊl〕n. 滿室   **under no circumstances** 絕不
deadline〔'dɛd,laɪn〕n. 截止時間
furiously〔'fjʊrɪəslɪ〕adv. （工作等）非常努力而迅速地

❖ Comprehension ❖

1. The professor told the students _____.
    (A) to do the best they could on the exam
    (B) to turn in their papers within two hours
    (C) that he would punish the students who cheated
    (D) not to hand in their papers until they were finished

2. After the deadline passed, _____.
    (A) one student continued to work
    (B) all of the students stopped working
    (C) the professor returned all the papers
    (D) the professor scolded the students

3. The slow student wanted to _____.
    (A) copy the other students' answers
    (B) make sure the professor didn't know him
    (C) finish his examination early and go home
    (D) destroy the other students' papers

4. The slow student said, "Terrific," because _____.
    (A) he was very angry at the professor
    (B) the professor wouldn't be able to recognize his paper
    (C) he felt very happy that he had finally finished the test
    (D) he found that he was taller than the professor

** **tardy** 〔'tɑrdɪ〕 *adj.* 延遲的   **approach**〔ə'protʃ〕*v.* 走近
   clutch〔klʌtʃ〕*v.* 抓住   ***draw oneself up*** 站直
   stature〔'stætʃɚ〕*n.* 身長   **terrific**〔tə'rɪfɪk〕*adj.* 極佳的
   stuff〔stʌf〕*v.* 塞進   ***turn in*** 交出（= *hand in*）

37 Changing Attitudes Toward Children

We do not value very highly the unquestioning obedience and respect which used to be demanded for children. Words like "meek" or "very obedient" tend to be used nowadays more in criticism than in praise.

The general feeling is that a parent's duty is to prove himself worthy of a child's respect, to inspire it rather than command it or expect it as a natural right; and for children, the emphasis is not so much on obedience and duty as on trust and love, not so much on humility as on moral courage and independence. Bringing up a child is felt to be a training in independence.

** **value** 〔'væljʊ〕 *v.* 重視
unquestioning 〔ʌn'kwɛstʃənɪŋ〕 *adj.* 不懷疑的;絕對的
obedience 〔ə'bidɪəns〕 *n.* 服從　　**meek** 〔mik〕 *adj.* 溫順的
criticism 〔'krɪtə,sɪzəm〕 *n.* 批評　　**inspire** 〔ɪn'spaɪr〕 *v.* 引發;喚起
humility 〔hju'mɪlətɪ〕 *n.* 謙卑
independence 〔,ɪndɪ'pɛndəns〕 *n.* 獨立

❖ Comprehension ❖

1. Today, children are expected to be _____.
   - (A) meek
   - (B) obedient
   - (C) respectful
   - (D) independent

2. In child-rearing, the emphasis is now on _____.
   - (A) criticism
   - (B) humility
   - (C) trust
   - (D) duty

3. Which expression best sums up the old attitudes?
   - (A) I'm okay, you're okay.
   - (B) You do your thing, I'll do mine.
   - (C) Children should be seen and not heard.
   - (D) Don't worry; be happy.

4. According to the above passage, today's parents _____.
   - (A) win respect from their children only if they are young
   - (B) cannot expect blind obedience and respect from their children
   - (C) tend to command respect from children
   - (D) prove unworthy of children's respect

** **rearing** 〔'rɪrɪŋ〕 *n.* 養育   ***sum up*** 簡略地說；概述

38 The Truth About Exercise

Physiologists used to believe that any type of physical activity was harmful to the man over forty. We doctors are to blame as much as anyone for warning patients over 40 to "take it easy" and give up golf and other forms of exercise. Twenty years ago one famous writer even suggested that any man over forty should never stand when he could sit, never sit when he could lie down — in order to "conserve" his strength and energy.

Physiologists and M. D.'s, including the nation's leading heart specialists, now tell us that activity, even strenuous activity, is not only permissible, but required for good health at any age. You are never too old to exercise.

** **physiologist**〔͵fɪzɪ'alədʒɪst〕 *n.* 生理學家
take it easy 放輕鬆　　**conserve**〔kən'sɜv〕 *v.* 保存
M. D. 醫學博士（= *Doctor of Medicine*）
specialist〔'speʃəlɪst〕 *n.* 專家　**strenuous**〔'strɛnjʊəs〕 *adj.* 費力的
permissible〔pə'mɪsəbl̩〕 *adj.* 可容許的　*engage in* 從事
participate in 參與　　*take up* 開始；從事

❖ Comprehension ❖

1. People over forty _____ .

    (A) have heart problems if they exercise
    (B) are permitted to be active if they are careful
    (C) should not engage in strenuous activity
    (D) should be active if they want to be healthy

2. The main idea of this paragraph is that _____ .

    (A) people should listen to their doctors' advice
    (B) strenuous exercise has been proven to be harmful to
        people over 40
    (C) physiologists have not always been correct in their
        advice about exercise
    (D) people over 40 should be careful about participating
        in exercise programs

3. A famous writer suggested that men over forty should
    _____ .

    (A) stand instead of sitting
    (B) save their energy whenever possible
    (C) take up golf
    (D) lie down every day

4. To be healthy, people should _____ .

    (A) take it easy
    (B) conserve their strength
    (C) exercise
    (D) avoid strenuous exercise

39 Jumping to Conclusions

In some degree, we all have some restricted professional vision. The tailor runs his eyes over your clothes and reckons you up according to the cut of your garments and the degree of shininess they display. The boot maker looks at your boots and takes your intellectual, social and financial measurement from their quality and condition.

It is so with the dentist. He judges all the world by its teeth. One look in your mouth and he has settled and immovable convictions about your character, your habits, your physical condition, your position, and your mental attributes.

** *jump to a conclusion* 遽下斷語
    restricted 〔rɪˈstrɪktɪd〕 *adj.* 受限制的　**vision** 〔ˈvɪʒən〕 *n.* 眼光
    reckon up 結算　　**garment** 〔ˈgɑrmənt〕 *n.* 衣服
    shininess 〔ˈʃaɪnɪnɪs〕 *n.* 光亮　　**display** 〔dɪˈsple〕 *v.* 展示
    financial 〔faɪˈnænʃəl〕 *adj.* 財務的
    measurement 〔ˈmɛʒəmənt〕 *n.* 測量　**settled** 〔ˈsɛtḷd〕 *adj.* 固定的
    conviction 〔kənˈvɪkʃən〕 *n.* 確信　**attribute** 〔ˈætrə,bjut〕 *n.* 本性
    intolerant 〔ɪnˈtɑlərənt〕 *adj.* 不寬容的

❖ Comprehension ❖

1. The main idea of this passage is that_____.

   (A) we should not judge people by appearances
   (B) professionals tend to be narrow-minded and intolerant
   (C) a person's profession influences the way he judges other people
   (D) it is best to be open-minded

2. The author's attitude toward the tendency he describes is_____.

   (A) strong disapproval   (B) reluctant acceptance
   (C) admiration   (D) not clear from the passage

3. What is meant by "It is so with the dentist."?

   (A) Dentists also pay attention to people's boots.
   (B) Boot makers also notice dentists' boots.
   (C) Dentists also use restricted professional vision in evaluating others.
   (D) Dentists also take intellectual, social and financial measurements.

4. A similar example might be a_____who judges people by their_____.

   (A) barber — hairstyle   (B) banker — wealth
   (C) teacher — intelligence   (D) judge — crimes

** **disapproval** 〔,dɪsə'pruvl̩〕 *n.* 不贊成
   reluctant 〔rɪ'lʌktənt〕 *adj.* 勉強的   **evaluate** 〔ɪ'væljʊ,et〕 *v.* 評價

40 Two Views of Marriage

She was writing to their son, congratulating him on his engagement.

"My darling boy," wrote the mother, "what glorious news! Your father and I rejoice in your happiness. It has long been our greatest wish that you should marry some good woman. A good woman is Heaven's most precious gift to man. She brings out all the best in him and helps him to suppress all that is evil."

Then there was a postscript in a different handwriting:

"Your mother has gone for a stamp. Keep single, you young fool."

** *congratulate sb. on sth.* 祝賀某人～
  engagement 〔ɪn'gedʒmənt〕 *n.* 訂婚
  glorious 〔'gloriəs〕 *adj.* 極好的　**rejoice** 〔rɪ'dʒɔɪs〕 *v.* 高興
  precious 〔'prɛʃəs〕 *adj.* 寶貴的　*bring out* 使顯現
  suppress 〔sə'prɛs〕 *v.* 抑制　**postscript** 〔'postskrɪpt〕*n.* 附筆(略作P.S.)
  handwriting 〔'hænd,raɪtɪŋ〕 *n.* 筆跡　**single** 〔'sɪŋgl〕 *adj.* 獨身的

◈ Comprehension ◈

1.　In her letter, the mother told her son_____.

    (A) that she was glad he was getting married

    (B) to think carefully before getting married

    (C) that she had to go to get a stamp

    (D) that he should buy his wife precious gifts

2.　The postscript on the letter_____.

    (A) was written by the boy's mother

    (B) was written by the boy's father

    (C) was written by the boy's fiancée

    (D) congratulated the son

3.　We assume that the father_____.

    (A) rejoiced in the good news

    (B) appreciated his wife

    (C) avoided all that is evil

    (D) regretted his marriage

4.　We assume that the mother_____.

    (A) nagged her husband

    (B) wished she had remained single

    (C) hoped her son would break his engagement

    (D) thought a husband was Heaven's gift to woman

** fiancée〔,fɪɑnˊse〕n. 未婚妻　　appreciate〔əˊpriʃɪ,et〕v. 感激
　nag〔næg〕v. 不停地嘮叨

41 An Unrecognized Vice

As of all other good things, one can have too much even of reading. Indulged in to excess, reading becomes a vice — a vice all the more dangerous, for not being generally recognized as such.

Yet excessive reading is the only form of self-indulgence which fails to get the blame it deserves. The fact is surprising; for it is obvious to anyone who candidly observes himself and other people that excessive reading can devour a man's time, dissipate his energies, vitiate his thinking and distract his attention from reality.

————*Aldous Huxley, "Proper Studies"*

** **vice**〔vaɪs〕 *n.* 不良習慣　　**indulge**〔ɪn'dʌldʒ〕 *v.* 沈溺於
　to excess 過度地（＝*too much*）　　**all the more** 更加；越發
　self-indulgence〔,sɛlfɪn'dʌldʒəns〕 *n.* 自我放縱
　deserve〔dɪ'zɝv〕 *v.* 應得　　**candidly**〔'kændɪdlɪ〕 *adv.* 誠實地
　devour〔dɪ'vaur〕 *v.* 吞沒　　**dissipate**〔'dɪsə,pet〕 *v.* 浪費
　vitiate〔'vɪʃɪ,et〕 *v.* 使失效　　**distract**〔dɪ'strækt〕 *v.* 轉移

❖ Comprehension ❖

1. What is meant by " As of all other good things "?
   (A) All things are good.
   (B) Reading is one of many good things.
   (C) Everything is good sometimes.
   (D) Only reading is a good thing.

2. Which statement is true according to the passage ?
   (A) Most bad habits are worse than reading is.
   (B) Too much reading is a waste of time.
   (C) Most people know that they read too much.
   (D) Reading helps people be happy.

3. The author thinks that_____ .
   (A) most people don't know that too much reading is harmful
   (B) most people know that too much reading is harmful
   (C) most people read too much on their holidays
   (D) most people never read enough to be hurt by it

4. The author thinks that reading_____ .
   (A) devours a man's time
   (B) dissipates man's energy
   (C) distracts man's attention from reality
   (D) is good within certain limits

** **Aldous Huxley** 奧爾德斯・赫胥黎 (英國小說家及評論家)

Appreciating Distance

I number it among my blessings that my father had no car ; although most of my friends had. The deadly power of rushing about wherever I pleased had not been given me. I measured distance by the standard of my own internal combustion engine. I had not been allowed to make little of the very idea of distance ; in return I possessed infinite riches in what would have been to motorists a small area. The truest and most horrible claim made for modern transport is that it "wipes out space." It does. It wipes out one of the most glorious gifts we have been given. It is a sort of bad inflation which lowers the value of distance, so that nowadays a young man may travel a hundred miles with less sense of liberation and pilgrimage and adventure than his grandfather got from travelling ten.

** **appreciate**〔ə'priʃɪ,et〕*v.* 重視；珍惜
number〔'nʌmbə〕*v.* 計入；算作　　**blessing**〔'blɛsɪŋ〕*n.* 幸福的事
deadly〔'dɛdlɪ〕*adj.* 極度的　　**internal**〔ɪn'tɜnl̩〕*adj.* 內部的

❖ Comprehension ❖

1. Because he didn't have a car, the author_____.
   (A) appreciates the value of hard work
   (B) was able to find rich meaning in a small area
   (C) always wanted his friends to take him for rides
   (D) feels a great sense of liberation when he drives

2. Rushing about in a car is described as_____.
   (A) liberation   (B) a pilgrimage
   (C) an adventure   (D) a deadly power

3. The author thinks that the idea that modern transport "wipes out space" is_____ .
   (A) true, and very unfortunate
   (B) not true, though many people claim it
   (C) exactly what his father believed
   (D) infinitely rich

4. To the author, space is_____.
   (A) a glorious gift   (B) an inconvenience
   (C) bad inflation   (D) of little value

** **combustion** 〔kəm'bʌstʃən〕 *n.* 燃燒   *make little of* 看不起
infinite 〔'ɪnfənɪt〕 *adj.* 無數的   **motorist** 〔'motərɪst〕 *n.* 開汽車者
claim〔klem〕 *n.* 聲明   **transport**〔'trænsport,-pɔrt〕 *n.* 運輸
wipe out 消滅   **inflation**〔ɪn'fleʃən〕 *n.* 誇張
liberation〔ˌlɪbə'reʃən〕 *n.* 解放
pilgrimage〔'pɪlgrəmɪdʒ〕 *n.* 朝聖

That's Perfect

In one of the scenes in a play, it was necessary to produce the effect of a wonderful sunset. But the director was a very difficult man to please, as he had his own very definite ideas of how the scene should look.

The theater electricians worked very hard to produce this sunset effect. They tried out all kinds of arrangements and combinations of lights — red lights, orange lights, yellow lights, blue lights, lights from above, lights from behind, lights from the front, lights from the sides — _____ , until suddenly the director saw exactly the effect that he had been dreaming of producing. "That's it！" he shouted excitedly to the electricians behind the stage. "Keep it exactly like that！" "I'm sorry, sir," answered the chief electrician, "but we can't." "Why not？" asked the director angrily. "Because the theater is on fire, sir," answered the chief electrician. "That's what's producing the effect you see now！"

❖ Comprehension ❖

1. Which one fits in the blank ?

   (A) and all of them were impressive
   (B) but nothing satisfied the director
   (C) and many of them were expensive
   (D) but they were mostly too dark

2. The director in this story_____.

   (A) is also an actor
   (B) is difficult to satisfy
   (C) is very frightened by fire
   (D) doesn't know much about drama

3. The electricians tried very hard to _____.

   (A) reduce the cost of the play
   (B) put out the fire
   (C) create the impression of a sunset
   (D) find a new playwright to write a play

4. The fire was probably caused by_____.

   (A) electricity   (B) cigarettes
   (C) explosives   (D) arson

** **scene**〔sin〕*n.*（戲劇的）一場；一景   **director**〔dəˈrɛktə〕*n.* 導演
   definite〔ˈdɛfənɪt〕*adj.* 一定的   **electrician**〔ɪ,lɛkˈtrɪʃən〕*n.* 電工
   try out 徹底試驗   **combination**〔,kɑmbəˈneʃən〕*n.* 組合
   be on fire 著火   **impressive**〔ɪmˈprɛsɪv〕*adj.* 給人深刻印象的
   put out 熄滅   **playwright**〔ˈple,raɪt〕*n.* 劇作家
   explosive〔ɪkˈsplosɪv〕*n.* 炸藥   **arson**〔ˈɑrsn̩〕*n.* 縱火

44 The Danger of Sensationalism

The newspaper and its public are very much like the boy who was always crying "wolf" and the people who soon learned not to pay any attention to him. When a newspaper pumps artificial excitement into its every item, eventually the public catches on to the trick and becomes surfeited. The reader sees a scary headline, and he thinks, "Just another newspaper story." Once in a while a story comes along which is a hundred times more important than its predecessors; one which should command the instant attention and thought of every reader. But the newspaper has no means of showing this unusual importance; it has been so much in the habit of using sensational language and headlines that those devices no longer have any special force.

** **sensationalism**〔sɛnˋseʃənḷˏɪzəm〕 *n.* 煽情主義
pump〔pʌmp〕 *v.* 注入　　**artificial**〔ˏɑrtəˋfɪʃəl〕 *adj.* 人爲的
item〔ˋaɪtəm〕 *n.* （新聞記事的）一則
eventually〔ɪˋvɛntʃʊəlɪ〕 *adv.* 最後　　***catch on to*** 瞭解
surfeit〔ˋsɝfɪt〕 *v.* 使人厭膩　　**scary**〔ˋskɛrɪ, ˋskærɪ〕 *adj.* 嚇人的

❖ Comprehension ❖

1. The author says that newspaper stories are often
   _____ .

   (A) factual
   (B) exaggerated
   (C) false
   (D) important

2. People often don't pay attention to important newspaper stories because _____ .

   (A) they aren't written well
   (B) the headlines frighten them
   (C) newspapers have already overused sensational lan-
       guage
   (D) they don't understand the language used

3. According to the passage, readers react to sensational
   language with _____ .

   (A) excitement　　　　(B) concern
   (C) attention　　　　(D) boredom

4. Which is an example of a device, as used here?

   (A) a newspaper　　　(B) an important story
   (C) a scary headline　(D) special force

** headline〔'hɛd,laɪn〕 *n.* （報紙上的）標題　　***come along*** 出現
   predecessor〔,prɛdɪ'sɛsɚ〕 *n.* 以前的東西
   command〔kə'mænd〕 *v.* 應得　　**device**〔dɪ'vaɪs〕 *n.* 方法
   exaggerated〔ɪg'zædʒə,retɪd〕 *adj.* 誇大的

45 An Encouraging Prediction

I was on the whole considerably discouraged by my school days. Except in fencing, in which I won the Public School Championship, I achieved no distinction. All my contemporaries and even younger boys seemed in every way better adapted for the conditions of our little world. They were far better both at the games and at the lessons. It is not pleasant to feel oneself so completely outclassed and left behind at the very beginning of the race. I was surprised on taking leave of Mr. Welldon, the principal of our school, to hear him predict with confidence that I should be able to succeed. I have always been very grateful to him for this.

** **prediction** 〔prɪ'dɪkʃən〕 *n.* 預測　　*on the whole* 就整體而言
　considerably 〔kən'sɪdərəblɪ〕 *adv.* 相當地
　discourage 〔dɪs'kɜɪdʒ〕 *vt.* 使沮喪　　**fencing** 〔'fɛnsɪŋ〕 *n.* 劍術
　distinction 〔dɪ'stɪŋkʃən〕 *n.* 優秀；卓越
　contemporary 〔kən'tɛmpə,rɛrɪ〕 *n.* 同年齡的人
　adapt 〔ə'dæpt〕 *vt.* 使適應　　**outclass** 〔aʊt'klæs〕 *v.* 超越
　leave ~ behind 超越~　　*take leave of* 向~告別
　principal 〔'prɪnsəpḷ〕 *n.* 校長

❖ Comprehension ❖

1. The author's winning of the fencing championship
   _____.

   (A) surprised Mr. Welldon
   (B) was one example of his impressive performances
   (C) was his only honor at school
   (D) discouraged his classmates

2. Which is true according to the passage?

   (A) He did better than his classmates.
   (B) He did well in both sports and studies.
   (C) He became adapted to the real world.
   (D) He was generally inferior to his classmates in sports and scholarship.

3. The author is thankful to Mr. Welldon for _____.

   (A) expressing confidence in his future success
   (B) helping him to win the fencing championship
   (C) allowing him to graduate despite his poor record
   (D) congratulating him on his success

4. The author found his school experience _____.

   (A) useful in helping him adapt to the world
   (B) boring, except for fencing
   (C) quite discouraging
   (D) typical of all his other experiences in life

** *be grateful to A for B* 因爲B而感謝A
   scholarship〔'skɑlɚ,ʃɪp〕 *n.* 學問

Dear Ann Landers

Overcoming a Phobia

Dear Ann Landers :

I am engaged to a wonderful girl. We plan to be married next year. She told me last night she hopes I don't mind sleeping with the lights on because all her life she has been afraid of the dark and can't seem to get over it.

I explained that the fear is all in her head and since I will be beside her there is nothing to be afraid of.

She's not a teenager, Ann, she's a grown woman. What can I do about it? I cannot sleep with the lights on. I tried it once and was up all night. Help me, please. — Panama City

Dear Panama :

All fears are in the head. What is needed is a technique for eliminating them. I suggest the gradual approach. First, a light in the closet or hall with the door left half-open. Then go to a dim night light. In the meantime, you might try wearing an eyeshade which can be bought in most drugstores. I hope I've helped.

❖ Comprehension ❖

1. The person writing to Ann Landers is _____.

   (A) afraid of sleeping with a woman
   (B) afraid of sleeping in the dark
   (C) planning to marry a woman who is afraid of the dark
   (D) trying to find out where he can buy an eyeshade

2. Ann Landers thinks that the _____.

   (A) woman will be able to get over her fear gradually
   (B) man should avoid marrying a woman with this problem
   (C) problem is big
   (D) woman should try wearing an eyeshade

3. Which is an example of " the gradual approach " ?

   (A) using eyeshades
   (B) sleeping with the lights on
   (C) getting married
   (D) using a night light

** **overcome**〔,ovə'kʌm〕 v. 克服   **phobia**〔'fobɪə〕 n. 恐懼症
  engage〔ɪn'gedʒ〕 v. 訂婚   ***get over*** 克服
  be up 睡不著的   **technique**〔tɛk'nik〕 n. 方法；技巧
  eliminate〔ɪ'lɪmə,net〕 v. 去除
  gradual〔'grædʒuəl〕 adj. 逐漸的   **approach**〔ə'protʃ〕 n. 方法
  closet〔'klɑzɪt〕 n. 衣櫥   **hall**〔hɔl〕 n. 走廊
  dim〔dɪm〕 adj. 微弱的   **eyeshade**〔'aɪ'ʃed〕 n. 眼罩
  in the meantime 其間；同時

46

Legal Aid

My husband, like many lawyers, gets late-evening phone calls, usually from someone who has been arrested. One night, though, the caller was an agitated female, and a snarling male voice could be heard in the background.

"If a man leaves his wife," the woman wanted to know, "doesn't she get the house and furniture?" My husband told her he did not give legal advice over the phone and asked her to call his office for an appointment.

The woman heard him out and then loudly replied, "Oh, you say she also gets the car, the boat and the savings account? Thank you very much." And triumphantly she hung up.

** legal〔ˋligḷ〕 *adj.* 法律的　　aid〔ed〕 *n.* 援助
　arrest〔əˋrɛst〕 *v.* 拘捕　　agitate〔ˋædʒə‚tet〕 *v.* 攪亂(心、感情)
　snarling〔ˋsnɑrlɪŋ〕 *adj.* 咆哮的　 *in the background* 在幕後；背地
　hear sb. out 聽某人說完　　savings account 儲蓄存款戶頭
　triumphantly〔traɪˋʌmfəntlɪ〕 *adv.* 得意洋洋地
　hang up 掛斷(電話)

◆ Comprehension ◆

1. The narrator_____.
   (A) works as a lawyer
   (B) owns a car and a boat
   (C) is married to a lawyer
   (D) wants to leave his wife

2. The " snarling male voice " belongs to_____.
   (A) the caller's dog
   (B) the lawyer
   (C) an unidentified stranger
   (D) the caller's husband

3. Late-night telephone calls to the narrator's house _____.
   (A) are fairly common
   (B) are extremely rare
   (C) cause great annoyance
   (D) are usually from angry women

4. The woman really telephoned in order to_____.
   (A) get useful legal advice
   (B) frighten the lawyer's wife
   (C) make her husband leave her
   (D) deceive her husband

** **unidentified**〔,ʌnaɪˈdɛntə,faɪd〕*adj.* 身分不明的

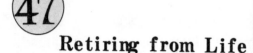

47 Retiring from Life

Many men go downhill rapidly after retirement. They feel that their active productive life is completed and their job is done. They have nothing to look forward to, become bored, inactive, and often suffer a loss of self-esteem because they feel left out of things, not important any more. They develop a self-image of a useless, worthless, "worn-out" hanger-on. And a great many die within a year or so after retirement.

It is not retiring from a job that kills these men, it is retiring from life. It is the feeling of uselessness, of being washed up; the dampening of self-esteem, courage and self-confidence.

** **go downhill** 走下坡；衰頹   **retirement**〔rɪ'taɪrmənt〕*n*. 退休
productive〔prə'dʌktɪv〕*adj*. 有生產力的
look forward to 期待   **self-esteem**〔‚sɛlfə'stim〕*n*. 自尊
self-image〔'sɛlf'ɪmɪdʒ〕*n*. 對自己的印象、想法
worn-out〔'wɔrn'aut〕*adj*. 疲憊不堪的
hanger-on〔'hæŋɚ'ɑn〕*n*. 依附他人者   **washed up** 完蛋的；沒有用的
dampen〔'dæmpən〕*v*. 減弱；使挫折

✧ Comprehension ✧

1. What does it mean to "go downhill"?

    (A) to take long, easy hikes
    (B) to take up jogging
    (C) to fail in power
    (D) to become useless

2. According to this paragraph many retired men _____ .

    (A) find second jobs
    (B) lead productive lives
    (C) feel useless
    (D) look forward to holidays

3. The author seems to feel that many retired men _____ .

    (A) are useless
    (B) feel happy
    (C) lose interest in life
    (D) are active

4. A great many men _____ within a year or two after retirement.

    (A) become worthless   (B) die
    (C) quit their jobs   (D) wash up

** **self-confidence** 〔ˈsɛlfˈkɑnfədəns 〕 *n*. 自信
   take up 從事；開始

How Italy Rediscovered Her Past

For a long time Rome had been the center of civilization, but after the Goths and Vandals attacked her in the fourth century A.D., the power of the Roman Empire was broken. The Italians, however, never forgot their country's great past, and they were always thinking how this greatness might return.

In 1453, Constantinople was taken by the Turks, and many Greek-speaking scholars who had been living there had to escape to the west. Many came to Italy, bringing with them ancient works of Greek literature which had been almost forgotten in Western Europe during the centuries since the end of the Roman Empire. The people of Italy became interested in what these scholars told them, and began to study the arts of the ancient world themselves. That, very briefly, is how the Renaissance began.

** **rediscover** 〔͵ridɪ'skʌvə〕 *vt.* 再發現
civilization 〔͵sɪvḷaɪ'zeʃən〕 *n.* 文明　　**Goth** 〔gɑθ〕 *n.* 哥德人
Vandal 〔'vændḷ〕 *n.* 汪達爾人　　**empire** 〔'ɛmpaɪr〕 *n.* 帝國

✦ Comprehension ✦

1. The Italians never forgot that _____ .
   (A) the Goths and Vandals had attacked Rome
   (B) the Goths and Vandals had no interest in Roman civilization
   (C) the Roman Empire was broken
   (D) Rome had once been the center of civilization

2. In 1453, Constantinople was conquered by_____ .
   (A) the Romans   (B) the Greeks
   (C) the Turks   (D) the Goths and Vandals

3. The Renaissance began because _____ .
   (A) people in Italy studied the arts of the ancient world
   (B) Italians wanted to return to Constantinople
   (C) people in Western Europe had almost forgotten the ancient works of Greek literature
   (D) some people had seen for a long time that it was coming

4. During the Renaissance, the Italians began to re-search_____out of national pride.
   (A) Greek literature   (B) Roman art
   (C) Gothic romance   (D) Turkish baths

** **Constantinople**〔ˌkɑnstæntəˈnopḷ〕 *n.* 君士坦丁堡
   be taken 被佔領（＝*be occupied*）　　**Turk**〔tɝk〕*n.* 土耳其人
   renaissance〔ˌrɛnəˈzɑns〕*n.* 復興（ the Renaissance 專指十四～十六
   世紀發生於歐洲之文藝復興 ）　　**research**〔riˈsɝtʃ〕*v.* 再尋找

Speak Up!

Make a habit of speaking more loudly than usual. Inhibited people are notoriously soft-spoken. Raise the volume of your voice. You don't have to shout at people and use an angry tone — just consciously practice speaking more loudly than usual. Loud talk in itself is a powerful disinhibitor.

Recent experiments have shown that you can exert up to 15% more strength, and lift more weight, if you shout, grunt or groan loudly as you make the lift. The explanation of this is that loud shouting disinhibits, and allows you to exert all your strength, including that which has been blocked off and tied up by inhibition.

** ***speak up*** 大聲說話　　**inhibit**〔ɪnˋhɪbɪt〕*v.* 抑制　　**inhibition** *n.*
notoriously〔noˋtorɪəslɪ〕*adv.* 聲名狼籍地
soft-spoken〔ˋsɔftˋspokən〕*adj.* 說話溫和的
volume〔ˋvɑljəm〕*n.* 音量　　**consciously**〔ˋkɑnʃəslɪ〕*adv.* 自覺地
disinhibitor〔͵dɪsɪnˋhɪbɪtɚ〕*n.* 消除壓抑之物
exert〔ɪgˋzɝt〕*v.* 運用　　**grunt**〔grʌnt〕*v.* 發出低沈的咕嚕聲

❖ Comprehension ❖

1. Inhibition_____ .
   (A) makes you stronger
   (B) blocks your strength
   (C) makes you angry
   (D) increases your abilities

2. Inhibited people are_____ soft-spoken.
   (A) fortunately
   (B) beautifully
   (C) well-known to be
   (D) never

3. People can lift heavy things if _____ .
   (A) they are happy
   (B) they shout when they lift
   (C) they have someone help them
   (D) they are inhibited

4. The main topic of this paragraph is_____ .
   (A) speaking loudly and clearly as a habit
   (B) using your voice to free yourself from inhibition
   (C) gaining strength through weight lifting
   (D) controlling your anger and saving your strength

** **groan**〔gron〕*v.* 呻吟　　***block off*** 阻塞
　　tie up 防礙　　***free oneself from***免除～

Save the Whales

Many of the world's people are concerned about the dwindling number of whales in the oceans and seas. People have hunted whales since about the eleventh century. Certain types of whales have been hunted too much. Recently, their numbers have decreased so much that they are in danger of becoming extinct.

Why do people want to save the whales? The reason is that whales help to keep a balance between plants and animals. People have disturbed this balance. People's sewage and garbage increase the amount of salt in ocean and sea water. The increased salt helps some plants and some very small animals to grow. These plants and animals can be harmful to fish. Whales eat enormous amounts of the plants and animals that thrive in very salty water. Therefore, whales are very important because they keep the ocean environment clean enough for fish.

** **whale** 〔hwel〕 *n.* 鯨　　***be concerned about*** 擔憂；關心
　　dwindle 〔'dwɪndl̩〕 *v.* 減少　　**extinct** 〔ɪk'stɪŋkt〕 *adj.* 絕種的
　　balance 〔'bæləns〕 *n.* 平衡　　**disturb** 〔dɪs'tɝb〕 *v.* 擾亂

◆ Comprehension ◆

1. Whales are gradually getting fewer because _____ .
   (A) many people are indifferent to them
   (B) the sea is overcrowed with fishes
   (C) they have been caught and killed for a long time
   (D) the sea has been terribly polluted

2. Sea water becomes _____ when wastes are thrown into it.
   (A) more fertile   (B) fit for whales to live in
   (C) hot   (D) salty

3. Whales are important because _____ .
   (A) people hunt them for food   (B) they are huge
   (C) they are in danger of becoming extinct
   (D) they help to keep a balance between plants and animals

4. The main topic of the above paragraph is _____ .
   (A) the reason people want to save the decreasing whales
   (B) wastes and sea pollution
   (C) hunting whales and their decreasing number
   (D) how salty water harms sea fish

** sewage〔'sjuɪdʒ〕 *n.* 下水道中之污物
   enormous〔ɪ'nɔrməs〕 *adj.* 極大的   thrive〔θraɪv〕 *v.* 繁盛
   indifferent〔ɪn'dɪfərənt〕 *adj.* 漠不關心的
   overcrowd〔,ovə'kraud〕 *v.* 過度擁擠
   fertile〔'fɝtl̩〕 *adj.* 肥沃的

A Polite Request

Dear Mr. Jones,

I wonder if you could help my wife and myself on a matter that has been troubling us increasingly during the last few weeks. We spend most of our evenings very quietly but are reluctant to complain about the noise from your radio which we usually hear, more loudly than you may realize, from about 7 o'clock until well after midnight. I wonder if you would be good enough to tone it down, particularly after 10 o'clock. We do both appreciate that in houses built as closely together as ours, it is difficult for some inconvenience not to be caused occasionally, but would both be grateful if something could be done because we are now, quite regularly, losing a good deal of necessary_____.

Yours sincerely,

Robert Newcomb

** **reluctant**〔rɪˈlʌktənt〕*adj.* 不願的
 tone down 將（收音機等的音量）放低

◆ Comprehension ◆

1. The above writing is a letter of _____ .

   (A) complaint (B) apology (C) thanks (D) appreciation

2. What troubles the writer and his wife ?

   (A) the noise from the neighbor's radio
   (B) shortage of money
   (C) unfriendliness of the neighbors
   (D) neighbors' indifference to them

3. What word best completes the last sentence ?

   (A) sleep (B) money (C) friendship (D) discomfort

4. According to the passage, which is true ?

   (A) The writer is on good terms with the neighbors.
   (B) The writer informs his neighbor that his wife is dying.
   (C) In the writer's neighborhood, houses are closely built.
   (D) The writer is thinking of moving away because of the inconvenience.

** appreciate〔ə'priʃɪ,et〕 v. 瞭解
   inconvenience〔,ɪnkən'vinjəns〕 n. 不方便
   occasionally〔ə'keʒənḷɪ〕 adv. 偶然地
   grateful〔'gretfəl〕 adj. 感謝的   regularly〔'rɛgjələlɪ〕 adv. 經常地
   sincerely〔sɪn'sɪrlɪ〕 adv. 誠懇地   apology〔ə'pɑlədʒɪ〕 n. 道歉
   discomfort〔dɪs'kʌmfət〕 n. 不舒服
   on good terms with 與～友善

On Edge

A business executive carries his work-a-day worries and his work-a-day "mood" home with him. All day he has been troubled, hurried, aggressive, and "set to go." Perhaps he has felt a bit of frustration which tends to make him irritable.

He stops working physically when he goes home. But he carries with him a residue of his aggressiveness, frustration, hurry and worry. He is still set to go and cannot relax. He is irritable with his wife and family. He keeps thinking about problems at the office, although there is nothing he can do about them.

** *on edge* 緊張的；急躁的   **executive**〔ɪgˈzɛkjʊtɪv〕 *n.* 經理主管級人員
mood〔mud〕 *n.* 心情   **hurried**〔ˈhɝɪd〕 *adj.* 匆忙的
aggressive〔əˈgrɛsɪv〕 *adj.* 積極的   **aggressiveness** *n.*
frustration〔frʌsˈtreʃən〕 *n.* 挫折
irritable〔ˈɪrətəbḷ〕 *adj.* 易怒的   **physically**〔ˈfɪzɪkḷɪ〕 *adv.* 身體上
residue〔ˈrɛzə‚dju〕 *n.* 殘餘   **relax**〔rɪˈlæks〕 *v.* 放鬆
overwork〔‚ovɚˈwɝk〕 *v.* 工作過度
interfere〔‚ɪntɚˈfɪr〕 *v.* 妨害

❖ Comprehension ❖

1. Businessmen don't know how to_____ .

   (A) work at home
   (B) solve problems in the office
   (C) leave work problems in the office
   (D) physically stop working

2. Which statement is true, according to the above story?

   (A) Businessmen like to relax at home with their wives and families.
   (B) Businessmen find it difficult to solve problems in their offices.
   (C) Businessmen carry their worries home and cannot relax.
   (D) Businessmen tend to be easily excited and frustrated in their work.

3. Businessmen find it hard to relax at home because _____ .

   (A) business is bad
   (B) they are overworked
   (C) they fight with their wives
   (D) they worry about business matters

4. The author of this passage might advise an executive to _____ .

   (A) take his work home with him
   (B) work overtime whenever possible
   (C) stay single so nothing interferes with his job
   (D) develop a hobby that lets him relax

Save the Sharks

Sharks are not as dangerous to humans as humans are to sharks. Even though millions of people venture into the oceans each year, fewer than fifty serious shark attacks occur on the average, and only ten of these are fatal. The reason for this low accident rate is that most sharks are afraid of creatures as large as humans. Of the 350 known species of sharks, only one — the great white shark — is totally unafraid of humans. Meanwhile, humans kill sharks in record numbers. Thousands are hunted and slain each year for food, or killed by underwater nets to protect swimmers. Even the great white shark is diminishing in number as humans hunt it for its teeth and jaws, which are sold as collectors' items. Maybe it is time we began worrying less about protecting people from sharks and more about protecting sharks from people.

** shark〔ʃɑrk〕*n.* 鯊魚　　venture〔'vɛntʃɚ〕*v.* 大膽去～
on the average 平均　　fatal〔'fetḷ〕*adj.* 致命的
species〔'spiʃɪz〕*n.* (生物分類上的)種

◆ Comprehension ◆

1. How many people are attacked by sharks each year ?
   - (A) millions
   - (B) thousands
   - (C) fewer than fifty
   - (D) record numbers

2. How many sharks are killed each year ?
   - (A) thousands
   - (B) fewer than fifty
   - (C) ten
   - (D) only one

3. The main reason that relatively few humans are killed by sharks is that_____.
   - (A) the great white sharks are hunted for their teeth and jaws
   - (B) most sharks are afraid of creatures as large as humans
   - (C) millions of people venture into the oceans each year
   - (D) humans kill sharks in record numbers

4. Why is the great white shark diminishing in number ?
   - (A) They are slain for food.
   - (B) They are killed to protect swimmers.
   - (C) They are attacked by smaller sharks.
   - (D) They are hunted for their teeth and jaws.

** meanwhile〔'min,hwaɪl〕*adv*. 另一方面   record〔'rɛkəd〕*adj*. 空前的
slain〔slen〕*v*. 殺害（slay 的過去分詞）
diminish〔də'mɪnɪʃ〕*v*. 減少   jaw〔dʒɔ〕*n*. 顎
collector〔kə'lɛktə〕*n*. 收藏者   relatively〔'rɛlətɪvlɪ〕*adv*. 比較上

The Mind as a Laboratory

When asked where his laboratory was, Einstein simply produced a fountain pen and said: "It is here."

He might more accurately have tapped his head and made the same comment, for his most significant contributions to science were not a product of the physics laboratory but the result of thought experiments performed entirely _____. Without such thought experiments it seems unlikely he could have achieved the insights which produced such marvelous progress in man's understanding of the physical world.

** **laboratory**〔ˈlæbrə͵torɪ〕 *n.* 實驗室　　**produce**〔prəˈdjus〕*v.* 拿出
fountain pen 鋼筆　　**accurately**〔ˈækjərɪtlɪ〕*adv.* 精確地
tap〔tæp〕*v.* 拍　　**comment**〔ˈkɑmɛnt〕*n.* 說明；評論
significant〔sɪgˈnɪfəkənt〕*adj.* 卓越的
contribution〔͵kɑntrəˈbjuʃən〕*n.* 貢獻
physics〔ˈfɪzɪks〕*n.* 物理學　　**perform**〔pəˈfɔrm〕*v.* 進行
insight〔ˈɪn͵saɪt〕*n.* 洞察力　　**marvelous**〔ˈmɑrvələs〕*adj.* 卓越的
physical〔ˈfɪzɪkl̩〕*adj.* 物質的

❖ Comprehension ❖

1. Which one best fits in the blank?
   (A) by his assistants
   (B) in his mind
   (C) by machines
   (D) without purpose

2. An example of a thought experiment would be_____.
   (A) measuring the speed of light
   (B) building an atomic bomb
   (C) imagining moving at the speed of light
   (D) writing a paper

3. The author stresses that Einstein was exceptional because he_____.
   (A) used a fountain pen, not a typewriter
   (B) was modest and humble
   (C) did not use an experimental laboratory
   (D) forgot the location of his laboratory

4. Einstein contributed to society by_____.
   (A) increasing our understanding of the physical world
   (B) developing creative laboratory experiments
   (C) producing a fountain pen
   (D) encouraging the work of his assistants

** stress〔strɛs〕 *v.* 強調   exceptional〔ɪkˈsɛpʃənḷ〕 *adj.* 特別的

Wake Them Up

A minister passed along to a beginning preacher a trick he used when he saw the congregation nodding a bit. " I suddenly say to them, 'Last night I held another man's wife in my arms." When everyone sits up, shocked, I continue, 'It was my own dear mother.' "

The young preacher thought he'd try it. The next Sunday when _____ were dozing, he said in a loud voice, "You know, last night I held another man's wife in my arms." Stunned, the congregation suddenly sat upright and stared, whereupon the preacher stammered, "Oh, dear — I've forgotten who she was."

** **minister** 〔'mɪnɪstə〕 *n.* 牧師　　***pass along*** *A to B* 把A傳給B
　 preacher 〔'pritʃə〕 *n.* 牧師；傳道者
　 congregation 〔,kɑŋgrɪ'geʃən〕 *n.* (參加禮拜儀式的) 會衆
　 nod 〔nɑd〕 *v.* 打瞌睡　　***sit up*** 坐直
　 doze 〔doz〕 *v.* 打瞌睡　　**stun** 〔stʌn〕 *vt.* 使嚇呆
　 upright 〔,ʌp'raɪt〕 *adj.* 直立的
　 whereupon 〔,hwɛrə'pɑn〕 *adv.* 於是；然後

❖ Comprehension ❖

1. Which of the following best fits in the blank ?

   (A) all the people in the town
   (B) most members of his congregation
   (C) the preacher and the minister
   (D) his wife and another man's wife

2. The minister gave the preacher advice on_____.

   (A) keeping his listeners awake
   (B) holding other men's wives
   (C) explaining religion to his congregation
   (D) preventing stammering

3. The purpose of the minister's trick was to_____.

   (A) make the congregation laugh
   (B) help the congregation to relax easily
   (C) wake the listeners by shocking them
   (D) steal other men's wives

4. As a result of the young preacher's mistake,_____.

   (A) everybody in the congregation fell asleep
   (B) he was forced to leave his job
   (C) he appeared to be a very evil man
   (D) he made his mother very angry

** **stammer** 〔'stæmɚ〕 *v*. 結巴地說   **religion**〔rɪ'lɪdʒən〕 *n*. 宗教
relax〔rɪ'læks〕 *v*. 放鬆

A Hidden Cause of Accidents

Insurance companies, and other agencies which do research on the causes of accidents, have found that emotional carry-over causes many automobile accidents. If the driver has just had an argument with his wife or his boss, if he has just experienced frustration, or if he has just left a situation which called for aggressive behavior, he is much more likely to have an accident. *He carries over into his driving attitudes and emotions which are inappropriate.* He is not really angry at the other drivers. He is somewhat like a man who wakes up in the morning from a dream in which he experienced extreme anger. He realizes that the injustice heaped upon him happened only in a dream. But he is still angry.

** **insurance** 〔 ɪnˈʃʊrəns 〕 *n.* 保險　　**agency** 〔ˈedʒənsɪ〕 *n.* 機構
research 〔ˈrisɝtʃ, rɪˈsɝtʃ 〕 *n.* 研究
emotional 〔 ɪˈmoʃənḷ 〕 *adj.* 情緒的　　**carry-over** 〔ˈkærɪˈovɚ 〕 *n.* 留存
frustration 〔 frʌsˈtreʃən 〕 *n.* 挫折　　***call for*** 需要
aggressive 〔 əˈgrɛsɪv 〕 *adj.* 攻擊性的

✥ Comprehension ✥

1. According to the passage, many automobile accidents
   are caused by_____ .
   (A) inexperienced drivers   (B) people who dream
   (C) emotions   (D) driving skill

2. Emotional carry-over means _____ .
   (A) to give sympathy to someone you care about
   (B) to be very angry at other drivers
   (C) to transfer feelings from one experience to another
   (D) to resist attempts to change your behavior

3. The researchers were investigating the causes of
   _____ .
   (A) auto accidents   (B) marital strife
   (C) injustice   (D) dreams

4. Which of the following words does not belong ?
   (A) frustration   (B) anger
   (C) experience   (D) aggression

** *carry over A into B* 把 A 延伸到 B
   inappropriate 〔͵ɪnə'proprɪɪt〕 *adj.* 不適當的
   injustice 〔ɪn'dʒʌstɪs〕 *n.* 不公平   *heap A upon B* 把 A 堆積在 B 上
   transfer 〔træns'fɝ〕 *n.* 移轉   **investigate** 〔ɪn'vɛstə͵get〕 *v.* 研究
   marital strife 夫妻爭吵   **belong** 〔bə'lɔŋ〕 *v.* 歸屬（同一類）

57 Choosing a Resort

It has been found in a recent survey that most people have roughly the same ideas about the ideal place for a holiday.

The availability of public transport played little part in the choice of a locality, even for those people who did not own a car. According to the survey, forty percent of the people interviewed gave scenery as the most important factor in determining where to go. Thirty-six percent were primarily affected in their choice by the facilities provided at the holiday resort. Visiting friends and climate were the next important factors.

** **resort** 〔rɪ'zɔrt〕 *n.* 度假地點　　**survey** 〔'sɜve, sə've〕 *n.* 調查
roughly 〔'rʌflɪ〕 *adv.* 大約　　**availability** 〔ə,velə'bɪlətɪ〕 *n.* 便利
transport 〔'trænsport, -pɔrt〕 *n.* 運輸　　**locality** 〔lo'kælətɪ〕 *n.* 地點
interview 〔'ɪntə,vju〕 *v.* 訪問　　**scenery** 〔'sinərɪ〕 *n.* 風景
factor 〔'fæktə〕 *n.* 因素　　**primarily** 〔'praɪ,merəlɪ〕 *adv.* 主要地
affect 〔ə'fɛkt〕 *v.* 影響　　**facility** 〔fə'sɪlətɪ〕 *n.* 〔常用*pl.*〕設備
spot 〔spɑt〕 *n.* 地點　　**consideration** 〔kən,sɪdə'reʃən〕 *n.* 因素

❖ Comprehension ❖

1. The survey measured people's attitudes toward _____ .
   (A) public transportation
   (B) interviews
   (C) vacation spots
   (D) friendship

2. " Affected " in this passage means the same as _____ .
   (A) influenced
   (B) hurt
   (C) attracted
   (D) loved

3. According to the survey, _____ was the most important consideration.
   (A) scenery
   (B) facilities
   (C) friends
   (D) climate

4. The survey concluded that _____ .
   (A) people without cars look for places with public transport
   (B) visiting friends is more of a factor than the facilities
   (C) for 36 percent, interviews determined where they would spend their vacations
   (D) most people have the same ideas about the ideal vacation spot

58

Theater as Catharsis

When you enter a theater, you leave the everyday world behind. You take your seat, the lights go down, and you are in a different world. By an act of will you accept this new world as real for the moment. You accept the characters on the stage or screen as real people and their problems as real problems. As you watch the play unfold, you lose yourself. You identify yourself with one of the characters. You suffer his defeats, you enjoy his triumphs. By the end of the play you have lived another person's life so intimately that your own cares have been forgotten. When you come back to them, they seem somewhat different. Aristotle called this effect a " catharsis."

** **catharsis** 〔kəˈθɑrsɪs 〕 *n.* 淨化（特指戲劇淨化感情的作用）
for the moment 暫時
character 〔ˈkærəktə〕 *n.* （小說、戲劇等中的）人物；角色
screen 〔skrin〕 *n.* 螢幕　　**unfold** 〔ʌnˈfold〕 *v.* 展開
identify A with B 把 A 與 B 融爲一體　**defeat** 〔dɪˈfit〕 *n.* 失敗
triumph 〔ˈtraɪəmf〕 *n.* 勝利；成功
intimately 〔ˈɪntəmɪtlɪ〕 *adv.* 衷心地
Aristotle 〔ˈærə,stɑtḷ〕 *n.* 亞里斯多德（希臘的哲學家）

❖ Comprehension ❖

1. The everyday world is the world of _____.
   (A) the theater
   (B) the movie
   (C) your day-to-day life
   (D) Aristotle

2. What is meant by the sentence which reads, " By an act of will ⋯ as real " ?
   (A) In the play, you will see the real world.
   (B) You decide to believe that the events of the play or movie are real.
   (C) The stage or screen will attract you.
   (D) With the lights going down, you will forget your new world.

3. How can you lose yourself in a movie?
   (A) By identifying with the characters.
   (B) By suffering through a character's defeats.
   (C) By enjoying a character's triumphs.
   (D) All of the above.

4. " Catharsis " means _____.
   (A) accepting what you see as real
   (B) forgetting your cares
   (C) sharing another person's life intimately
   (D) none of the above

Two National Characters

The steadiness of English society, a necessary consequence of aristocratic institutions and habits, makes the English generally reserved and not easily excitable. The same cause gives stability to their views and inclinations. They are slow to promise, but you can depend upon them; they generally keep their word. It is difficult to get an English friend, but he remains a friend for life.

The American character is more amiable, frank, anxious to oblige, and ready to make friends. In the fullness of their heart, Americans generally promise more than they keep. Easily excited, they are not seldom deceived by their impressions, which, therefore, are often only transient.

** **steadiness** 〔'stɛdɪnɪs〕 *n.* 一成不變
consequence 〔'kɑnsə,kwɛns〕 *n.* 結果
aristocratic 〔,ærɪstə'krætɪk〕 *adj.* 貴族的
institution 〔,ɪnstə'tjuʃən〕 *n.* 制度　**reserved** 〔rɪ'zɜvd〕 *adj.* 內向的
stability 〔stə'bɪlətɪ〕 *n.* 穩定　**inclination** 〔,ɪnklə'neʃən〕 *n.* 嗜好
be slow to 不輕易　*keep one's word* 守約
amiable 〔'emɪəbl̩〕 *adj.* 親切的　**anxious** 〔'æŋʃəs〕 *adj.* 渴望的

◈ **Comprehension** ◈

1. This paragraph＿＿＿＿.
   (A) criticizes the English aristocracy
   (B) contrasts the English and American national characters
   (C) explains why America is technologically ahead of Britain
   (D) urges the reader to be more frank and amiable

2. Americans are less reserved because＿＿＿＿.
   (A) their country lacks a tradition of aristocracy
   (B) they don't worry about keeping promises
   (C) they are often deceived by impressions
   (D) they are anxious to oblige

3. An American friend is probably＿＿＿＿than an English one, according to this paragraph.
   (A) more difficult to get to know
   (B) easier to make, but less trustworthy
   (C) more reliable and steady
   (D) less kind and generous

4. In making promises, friends, and judgements,＿＿＿＿.
   (A) the English are quicker than the Americans
   (B) we should all be more careful
   (C) the Americans are quicker than the English
   (D) aristocrats tend to be extremely intelligent

** **oblige** 〔ə'blaɪdʒ〕 *v*.爲人盡力　*in the fullness of one's heart* 滿腔熱情
deceive 〔dɪ'siv〕 *v*. 欺騙　**transient** 〔'trænʃənt〕 *adj*.瞬間的;易變的

60

Reducing Anxiety

A great many worries can be diminished by realizing the unimportance of the matter which is causing the anxiety.

I have done in my time a considerable amount of public speaking; at first every audience terrified me, and nervousness made me speak very badly. I dreaded the ordeal so much that I always hoped I might break my leg before I had to make a speech, and when it was over I was exhausted from the nervous strain.

Gradually I taught myself to feel that it did not matter whether I spoke well or ill, the universe would remain much the same in either case.

I found that the less I cared whether I spoke well or badly, the less badly I spoke, and gradually the nervous strain diminished almost to vanishing point. A great deal of nervous fatigue can be dealt with in this way. Our doings are not so important as we naturally suppose; our successes and failures do not after all_____.

** **anxiety** 〔æŋ'zaɪətɪ〕 *n.* 焦慮　　**diminish** 〔də'mɪnɪʃ〕 *v.* 減少
considerable 〔kən'sɪdərəbḷ〕 *adj.* 不少的

✦ Comprehension ✦

1. Which of the following best completes the last sentence?
   (A) make us so nervous   (B) matter very much
   (C) exhaust us so much   (D) last for a long time

2. This passage gives advice on how to_____ .
   (A) avoid worry and nervousness
   (B) avoid breaking a leg
   (C) be a good public speaker
   (D) deal with fatigue and exhaustion

3. This passage advises us to _____ .
   (A) be less worried about successes and failures
   (B) try our best in every situation
   (C) be careful to speak well in public
   (D) avoid speaking in public

4. According to this passage, the things that worry us_____ .
   (A) are constantly changing
   (B) aren't as important as they seem
   (C) make good topics for speeches
   (D) are essential to our successes

** **audience** 〔'ɔdɪəns〕 *n*. 聽衆;觀衆   **dread** 〔drɛd〕 *v*. 害怕
   ordeal 〔ɔr'dil〕 *n*. 痛苦的考驗   **exhaust** 〔ɪg'zɔst〕 *v*. 使力竭
   nervous 〔'nɝvəs〕 *adj*. 神經的;緊張的   **strain** 〔stren〕 *n*. 緊張
   universe 〔'junə,vɝs〕 *n*. 世界;宇宙   **vanish** 〔'vænɪʃ〕 *v*. 消失
   fatigue 〔fə'tig〕 *n*. 疲乏   ***deal with*** 應付
   doing 〔'duɪŋ〕 *n*. 所做所爲   **constantly** 〔'kɑnstəntlɪ〕 *adv*. 經常地

Dear Ann Landers

A Pleasant Problem

Dear Ann Landers:

This letter is not a joke. I look like Paul New-man, and it is ruining my life. I'm 30, happily married, the father of three children, and a steady churchgoer. The girl who runs the elevator in this building takes me down to the basement, pushes the stop button and tries to get friendly. The babysitter keeps asking me to kiss her good-night when I drive her home. When I stop at a lunch counter, women come over and ask for my autograph. Yesterday my wife saw me having a cup of coffee with a beautiful young girl from the office who has been making a pest of herself lately. I may be in a little trouble at home. Please help. — Case of Mistaken Identity

Dear Case:

If this is really a problem for you, you could deli-berately make yourself look unattractive. Try an ugly haircut or unfashionable clothes. But I think a thirty-year-old man should be able to avoid becoming involved in relationships he doesn't want. It isn't really very hard to let people know you're not romantically interested in them.

❖ Comprehension ❖

1. The man's problem is that _____ .
   (A) he isn't very attractive to women
   (B) he is too attractive to women
   (C) his wife doesn't trust him
   (D) he is strongly attracted to young girls

2. In what way is the writer like Paul Newman?
   (A) fame   (B) acting ability
   (C) good looks   (D) happy marriage

3. Ann Landers thinks that the man _____ .
   (A) probably isn't as handsome as he claims to be
   (B) could discourage the women's advances if he wanted to
   (C) might need to get professional help for his problem
   (D) is playing a joke on her

** **steady** ﹝'stɛdɪ﹞ *adj.* 固定的
　　churchgoer ﹝'tʃɝtʃ,goɚ﹞ *n.* 經常按時上教堂做禮拜的人
　　elevator ﹝'ɛlə,vetɚ﹞ *n.* 電梯
　　lunch counter (在長櫃枱上用餐的) 速簡餐廳
　　autograph ﹝'ɔtə,græf﹞ *n.* 親筆簽名
　　pest ﹝pɛst﹞ *n.* 令人討厭的人或物　　**identity** ﹝aɪ'dɛntətɪ﹞ *n.* 身分
　　deliberately ﹝dɪ'lɪbərɪtlɪ﹞ *adv.* 刻意地
　　unattractive ﹝,ʌnə'træktɪv﹞ *adj.* 無吸引力的
　　unfashionable ﹝ʌn'fæʃənəbl̩﹞ *adj.* 不時髦的
　　discourage ﹝dɪs'kɝɪdʒ﹞ *v.* 使氣餒　　**advances** ﹝əd'vænsɪz﹞ *n.pl.* 接近
　　professional ﹝prə'fɛʃənl̩﹞ *adj.* 專業的　　***play a joke on*** 捉弄

61

A Willful Misunderstanding

With luncheon guests due to arrive at any minute, my wife discovered that we were almost completely out of bread. I suggested we send our six-year-old Kathy to the store to get some.

"Here's a dollar," my wife said. "Get two loaves of sliced sandwich bread, if they have it. If they don't have it, get anything. But hurry!"

Kathy dashed off, and we waited—and waited. Finally she danced into view around the corner, a bright red—and obviously new—hula hoop whirling around her middle.

"Kathy!" her mother cried, "Where did you get that hula hoop—and where's the bread I sent you for?"

"Well, they didn't have sliced sandwich bread—" answered Kathy, "—and you said," she reminded us indignantly, "If they don't have that, get anything!"

** **willful**〔ˈwɪlfəl〕*adj.* 蓄意的　　**luncheon**〔ˈlʌntʃən〕*n.* 午餐
　　due to-V 預定～　　　　*out of* 用完～
　　loaves〔lovz〕*n.* 一條麵包（ loaf 的複數)
　　sliced〔slaɪst〕*adj.* 切片的　　*dash off* 衝出去
　　hula hoop 呼拉圈

❖ Comprehension ❖

1. Kathy was sent for_____ .
   (A) a hula hoop
   (B) bread
   (C) guests
   (D) money

2. The family needed sliced sandwich bread because_____ .
   (A) it was time for supper
   (B) they were hungry
   (C) they had invited guests over
   (D) their daughter liked it

3. What does the mother mean by saying "anything"?
   (A) a hula hoop
   (B) sandwich bread
   (C) any kind of bread
   (D) anything Kathy wants to have

4. Kathy bought a hula hoop because_____ .
   (A) she was asked to do so by her mother
   (B) a shopkeeper asked her to do so
   (C) she forgot what she had to do
   (D) she misunderstood what her mother said

** **whirl** 〔hwɜl〕 *v.* 旋轉   **middle** 〔'mɪdl̩〕 *n.* 腰部
   send A for B 派 A 去拿 B   **indignantly**〔ɪn'dɪgnəntlɪ〕 *adv.* 憤慨地

62 Practice Without Pressure

Some athletes practice in private with as little pressure as possible. They, or their coaches, refuse to permit the press to witness practice sessions, and even refuse to give out any information concerning their practice for publicity purposes, in order to protect themselves from pressure. Everything is arranged _____. The result is that they go into the crisis of actual competition without appearing to have any nerves at all. They become "human icicles," immune to pressure, not worrying about how they will perform, but depending upon "muscle memory" to execute the various motions which they have learned.

** **pressure** 〔'prɛʃɚ〕 *n.* 壓力 **in private** 私底下
   coach 〔kotʃ〕 *n.* 教練 **the press** 新聞界
   witness 〔'wɪtnɪs〕 *v.* 看到 **session** 〔'sɛʃən〕 *n.* 活動
   give out 發表；公布 **concerning** 〔kən'sɝnɪŋ〕 *prep.* 有關 (=*about*)
   publicity 〔pʌb'lɪsətɪ〕 *n.* 宣傳 **crisis** 〔'kraɪsɪs〕 *n.* 緊要關頭
   competition 〔,kɑmpə'tɪʃən〕 *n.* 比賽
   nerve 〔nɝv〕 *n.* 〔常用 *pl.*〕神經過敏 **icicle** 〔'aɪsɪkl̩〕 *n.* 冰柱
   immune 〔ɪ'mjun〕 *adj.* 免疫的 **muscle** 〔'mʌsl̩〕 *n.* 肌肉
   execute 〔'ɛksɪ,kjut〕 *v.* 執行

❖ Comprehension ❖

1. Which of the following fits in the blank?
   (A) by the coaches, publicity agents, and training staff
   (B) long before the start of the real competition
   (C) to make training and practice as relaxed as possible
   (D) to provide for the comfort and safety of the athletes

2. This paragraph describes what athletes do to prevent
   _____.
   (A) being injured during training
   (B) becoming nervous or worried
   (C) unfavorable publicity
   (D) injuring themselves in competition

3. A person with " no nerve " is free of _____.
   (A) skill
   (B) pressure
   (C) publicity
   (D) emotions

4. These athletes are called " human icicles " because they
   _____.
   (A) have a " cool " attitude when they compete
   (B) are very strong and hard in competition
   (C) have muscles with long "memories "
   (D) do not want any form of publicity

** staff〔stæf〕*n.* 全體人員   cool〔kul〕*adj.* 冷靜的

63 That's Thin Enough

A New Jersey attorney was delighted when his wife started to diet under her physician's direction. She was five feet four inches tall, weighed 212 pounds, and had alarmingly high blood pressure.

In ten months the wife became a shapely, attractive woman. The attorney was so pleased that he took her into New York City to buy a fur coat. Unfortunately, the salesman was also impressed with her looks. His hands kept caressing her shoulders as he helped her in and out of each coat.

The attorney was furious that his wife was now so appealing to other men. He insisted that she stop dieting. "You're thin enough," he said. He started taking her out to expensive restaurants for big dinners. He didn't stop his campaign until she was up over 299 pounds again.

** **attorney** 〔ə'tɜnɪ〕 *n.* 律師　　**diet** 〔'daɪət〕 *v.* 照規定飲食
physician 〔fə'zɪʃən〕 *n.* 醫生　　**alarmingly** 〔ə'lɑrmɪŋlɪ〕 *adv.* 驚人地
blood pressure 血壓　　**shapely** 〔'ʃeplɪ〕 *adj.* 身材勻稱的
be impressed with 對～留下深刻印象　**caress** 〔kə'rɛs〕 *vt.* 撫摸
appealing 〔ə'pilŋ〕 *adj.* 令人心動的　**campaign** 〔kæm'pen〕 *n.* 作戰行動

❖ Comprehension ❖

1. At the start of this story, the attorney's wife_____.
   - (A) wanted to buy a fur coat
   - (B) refused to go on a diet
   - (C) was extremely overweight
   - (D) was shapely and attractive

2. The woman's diet was _____.
   - (A) completely successful
   - (B) against her doctor's advice
   - (C) very expensive
   - (D) alarming

3. When they bought a fur coat, the attorney became
   angry because _____.
   - (A) it was too expensive
   - (B) his wife started eating and became fat again
   - (C) the salesman was attracted to his wife
   - (D) the salesman was not helpful

4. In the end, the attorney decided that_____.
   - (A) the fur coat was not too expensive
   - (B) he preferred his wife to be fat
   - (C) it was wonderful to have an attractive wife
   - (D) restaurants had become too expensive

** **overweight** 〔'ovɚ'wet〕 *adj.* 過重的

Spare the Rod …?

My father never beat us, and whether he was unlike his neighbors in that, I cannot say. A distant relation of ours, a brave and pious man, called Willie, beat his family mercilessly. My father regretted his harshness, and often told of a day when he had been walking home from church with Willie and another man, talking of their children, when the other man turned to Willie and said, "Never lift your hand to a child in anger. Wait, and you may change your mind." My father admired these words, and often repeated them. Yet Willie went on thrashing his family; why I do not know; perhaps in a sort of panic, terrified of what might happen to them if the evil were not driven out of them.

** **spare** 〔spɛr〕 *v.* 惜用　　**rod** 〔rɑd〕 *n.* 教鞭
　 distant 〔'dɪstənt〕 *adj.* 遠房的　　**relation** 〔rɪ'leʃən〕 *n.* 親戚
　 pious 〔'paɪəs〕 *adj.* 虔誠的　　**mercilessly** 〔'mɝsɪlɪslɪ〕 *adv.* 殘忍地
　 regret 〔rɪ'grɛt〕 *v.* 對~感到遺憾　　**harshness** 〔'hɑrʃnɪs〕 *n.* 嚴厲
　 thrash 〔θræʃ〕 *v.* 打　　**panic** 〔'pænɪk〕 *n.* 恐懼
　 drive A out of B 把A從B中驅除　　**treat** 〔trit〕 *v.* 對待（人）

⇨ **Spare the rod and spoil the child.** 〔諺〕孩子不打不成器。

❖ Comprehension ❖

1. This passage contrasts_____ with Willie's.

    (A) the author's attitudes toward religion

    (B) the author's father's way of treating children

    (C) the author's father's children

    (D) the author's reactions to the other man's words

2. Willie and the author's father were_____.

    (A) father and son

    (B) distant relatives

    (C) neighbors

    (D) brothers

3. "Never lift your hand to a child in anger." means _____.

    (A) never hit a child when you are angry

    (B) never scold a child

    (C) never push an angry child

    (D) never hit an angry child

4. The author seems to_____.

    (A) respect his father's attitude and admire his behavior

    (B) respect Willie's children more than the other man

    (C) be frightened of what happens to children who are evil

    (D) be a deeply religious man

A Practical Suggestion

An employer had spent a great deal of money to ensure that his men should work under the best conditions.

"Now, whenever I enter the workshop," he said, "I want to see every man cheerfully performing his task, and therefore I invite you to place in this box any further suggestions as to how that can be brought about."

A week later the box was opened; it contained only one slip of paper, on which was written: "Don't wear rubber heels when you enter the workshop."

** **employer** 〔ɪmˈplɔɪə〕 *n.* 老板　　**ensure** 〔ɪnˈʃʊr〕 *v.* 確保
conditions 〔kənˈdɪʃənz〕 *n. pl.* 環境
workshop 〔ˈwɜk͵ʃɑp〕 *n.* 工廠　　**perform** 〔pəˈfɔrm〕 *v.* 做
further 〔ˈfɜðə〕 *adj.* 另外的　　***bring about*** 導致
slip 〔slɪp〕 *n.* 紙片　　**rubber** 〔ˈrʌbə〕 *n.* 橡膠
heel 〔hil〕 *n.* 鞋的後跟　　**improvement** 〔ɪmˈpruvmənt〕 *n.* 改善
neatly 〔ˈnitlɪ〕 *adv.* 整潔地　　**code** 〔kod〕 *n.* 規定

❖ Comprehension ❖

1. The employer was very much concerned about the _____ .

   (A) financial success of his company
   (B) working conditions of his employees
   (C) quality of his company's products
   (D) public image of his company

2. The employer placed a box in the workshop so that _____ .

   (A) employees could suggest ideas for improvements
   (B) garbage could be removed neatly
   (C) money could be collected for poor people
   (D) he could enter the workshop more easily

3. Why was the boss given the advice, "Don't wear rubber heels when you enter the workshop." ?
   (A) Because the employee doesn't want to be secretly watched by the employer.
   (B) Because rubber heels don't look well on the employer.
   (C) Because rubber heels make a terrible noise when the employer walks.
   (D) Because rubber heels are used only by the employees.

4. The note implied that _____ .
   (A) the boss was spending too much
   (B) the conditions were miserable
   (C) no amount of improvements could make the workers cheerful
   (D) the dress code was too strict

66 Training Elephants

Two main techniques have been used for training elephants, which we may call respectively the tough and the gentle.

The former method simply consists of setting an elephant to work and beating him until he does what is expected of him. Apart from any moral considerations, this is a stupid method of training, for it produces a resentful animal who at a later stage may well turn man-killer.

The gentle method requires more patience in the early stages, but produces a cheerful, good-tempered elephant who will give many years of loyal service.

** **technique** 〔tɛkˊnik〕 *n.* 方法;技巧   **respectively** 〔rɪˊspɛktɪvlɪ〕 *adv.* 分別地
   tough 〔tʌf〕 *adj.* 嚴厲的   **former** 〔ˊfɔrmɚ〕 *adj.* 前者的
   consist of 由~組成   ***set ~ to-V*** 使~從事於
   expect A of B 要求A做B   ***apart from*** 除~之外
   moral 〔ˊmɔrəl〕 *adj.* 道德的   **resentful** 〔rɪˊzɛntfḷ〕 *adj.* 仇恨的
   stage 〔stedʒ〕 *n.* 時期;階段   ***may well*** 或許;可能
   good-tempered 〔ˊgʊdˊtɛmpɚd〕 *adj.* 好脾氣的;性格溫和的
   loyal 〔ˊlɔjəl〕 *adj.* 忠心耿耿的

❖ Comprehension ❖

1. Which is meant by the word "respectively"?
   (A) separately and in the order mentioned
   (B) for showing great respect
   (C) deserving great respect
   (D) combining two separate parts

2. What does the former method result in?
   (A) a lazy elephant
   (B) a hard-worker
   (C) a good-tempered elephant
   (D) a man-killer

3. "Apart from any moral considerations" means _____.
   (A) the technique is normally wrong
   (B) the animal has no moral sense
   (C) morality may be taught
   (D) without considering whether the action is moral

4. The author probably supports _____.
   (A) beating elephants
   (B) breeding resentment
   (C) training elephants with gentleness
   (D) creating man-killers

** separately〔'sɛpərɪtlɪ〕adv. 個別地   mention〔'mɛnʃən〕v. 提及
breed〔brid〕v. 引起；招致

67 Watch Closely!

A professor, in order to teach the value of observation, prepared a cupful of kerosene, mustard and castor oil, and calling the attention of the class, dipped a finger into the atrocious mixture and then sucked his finger. He next passed the mixture round to the students, who all did the same with the result that each got a nasty taste in his mouth.

When the cup returned and he observed the faces of his students, he remarked: "Gentlemen, I am afraid you did not use your powers of observation. The finger that I put into the cup was not the same one that I put in my mouth."

** **observation** 〔,ɑbzɚ'veʃən〕 *n.* 觀察　　**cupful** 〔'kʌp,fʊl〕 *n.* 一杯的量
　　kerosene 〔'kɛrə,sin, ,kɛrə'sin〕 *n.* 煤油
　　mustard 〔'mʌstɚd〕 *n.* 芥末　　**castor oil** 蓖麻油
　　dip 〔dɪp〕 *v.* 沾；浸　　**atrocious** 〔ə'troʃəs〕 *adj.* 壞透的；惡劣的
　　mixture 〔'mɪkstʃɚ〕 *n.* 混合物　　**suck** 〔sʌk〕 *v.* 舔；吸吮
　　nasty 〔'næstɪ〕 *adj.* 令人作嘔的　　**remark** 〔rɪ'mɑrk〕 *v.* 說
　　stress 〔strɛs〕 *v.* 強調　　**respectful** 〔rɪ'spɛktfəl〕 *adj.* 恭敬的

❖ Comprehension ❖

1. The professor was trying to _____ .
   (A) frighten his students
   (B) develop a new chemical mixture
   (C) stress the importance of observing carefully
   (D) punish his students by making them sick

2. The professor _____ .
   (A) liked the taste of the mixture
   (B) did not really taste the mixture
   (C) tasted a different mixture from the one he gave his students
   (D) was pretending to be a doctor

3. The students had not observed _____ .
   (A) that the mixture had a bad taste
   (B) that the professor had changed the mixture
   (C) which finger the professor sucked
   (D) the rules of polite behavior

4. The professor wanted his students to _____ .
   (A) study harder
   (B) be more polite and respectful
   (C) notice details more carefully
   (D) create their own mixtures

68 Over-Motivation

Persons who have to learn how to get out of a burning building will normally require two or three times as long to learn the proper escape route as they would if no fire were present. Some of them do not learn at all. Over-motivation interferes with reasoning processes. The automatic reaction mechanism is jammed by too much conscious effort — trying too hard. Something akin to " purpose tremor" develops and the ability to think clearly is lost. The ones who do manage somehow to get out of the building have learned a narrow fixed response. Put them in a different building, or change the circumstances slightly, and they react as badly the second time around as the first.

** **motivation**〔͵motə'veʃən〕*n*. 動機　　**route**〔rut〕*n*. 路線
interfere〔͵ɪntə'fɪr〕*v*. 阻礙　　**reasoning**〔'rizənɪŋ〕*n*. 推理
automatic〔͵ɔtə'mætɪk〕*adj*. 無意識的
mechanism〔'mɛkə͵nɪzm̩〕*n*.（心理學用語）機構
jam〔dʒæm〕*v*. 因故障而停頓　　*akin to* 類似
tremor〔'trɛmɚ〕*n*. 顫抖　　**develop**〔dɪ'vɛləp〕*v*. 出現
somehow〔'sʌm͵haʊ〕*adv*. 以某種方法

◈ Comprehension ◈

1. Which does NOT interfere with thinking?
   (A) over-motivation
   (B) the automatic reaction mechanism
   (C) purpose tremor
   (D) excessive conscious effort

2. Those who manage to escape would probably fail to do
   so if_____.
   (A) they were not afraid
   (B) they knew the escape route
   (C) they had learned a fixed, narrow response
   (D) they were in a different building

3. People who have an urgent need to learn something
   _____.
   (A) learn it quickly and don't forget it
   (B) do not learn efficiently
   (C) tend to be narrow-minded
   (D) are able to reason very clearly

4. This paragraph leads us to conclude that people learn
   _____.
   (A) best when they have a very strong motivation
   (B) at almost the same rate in all circumstances
   (C) better when they are young than when they get older
   (D) best when they are not trying too hard

** excessive 〔ɪk'sɛsɪv〕 *adj*. 過度的
   efficiently 〔ə'fɪʃəntlɪ〕 *adv*. 有效率地

Mayan Mathematics

The mathematics of the Mayans of Mexico was superior when compared to other less primitive cultures. They were familiar with the idea of zero nearly 1,000 years before the concept reached Europe through Arab traders who had opened up caravan routes across the deserts of the Middle East.

The Greeks wrote numbers by using letters of the alphabet, and the Romans had a difficult system which required writing four figures (Ⅷ) to express the number 8. Both cultures were unable to deal with large numbers with the ease that the Mayans could. The Mayans, in contrast, could express any number by the use of three symbols: the dot, the bar or dash, and a shell shape for zero.

** **Mayan**〔'majən〕*adj.* 馬雅的　*n.* 馬雅人　**superior**〔sʊ'pɪrɪə〕*adj.* 較好的
primitive〔'prɪmətɪv〕*adj.* 原始的　　**concept**〔'kɑnsɛpt〕*n.* 觀念
Arab〔'ærəb〕*adj.* 阿拉伯人的　　**trader**〔'tredə〕*n.* 商人
caravan〔'kærə,væn〕*n.* 旅行隊　　**alphabet**〔'ælfə,bɛt〕*n.* 字母
symbol〔'sɪmbḷ〕*n.* 符號　　**dot**〔dɑt〕*n.* 點　　**bar**〔bɑr〕*n.* 直線
dash〔dæʃ〕*n.* 橫線　　**advanced**〔əd'vænst〕*adj.* 進步的
organization〔,ɔrgənaɪ'zeʃən〕*n.* 結構　　**handle**〔'hændḷ〕*v.* 處理

◈ Comprehension ◈

1. The main idea of this paragraph is that _____ .
   (A) the Mayans were familiar with the idea of zero before many other cultures
   (B) the Greeks wrote numbers by using the alphabet
   (C) the Mayans could express any number by using only three symbols
   (D) the Mayans had advanced mathematics compared to other cultures

2. The primary method of organization of this paragraph is _____ .
   (A) definition   (B) reasons
   (C) process   (D) comparison and contrast

3. Mayan mathematics was superior to Roman and Greek mathematics because _____ .
   (A) the Mayans had more contact with traders from the Middle East
   (B) the Mayan zero was a more elegant shape
   (C) the Mayans were able to handle large numbers more easily
   (D) the Mayan system used a larger number of symbols

4. The phrase " Both cultures " refers to_____ .
   (A) Greeks and Romans
   (B) Europeans and Arabs
   (C) Mexicans and Mayans
   (D) primitive and advanced cultures

A Heroic Nurse

　　Clara Louise Maass was a nurse who contributed to the research on yellow fever at the turn of the century. She was working as a civilian nurse in Cuba, where army Majors William Gorgas and Walter Reed were conducting experiments to isolate the cause of the disease. Tests ruled out dirt and poor sanitation as causes of yellow fever, and a mosquito was the suspected carrier. Clara was among the group who volunteered to be bitten by the insect. She contracted the disease and died on August 24, 1901. She was the only woman to participate in the experiment and among the few volunteers to die from it. With her death, the study ended; the results of the experiment provided conclusive evidence that mosquitoes were the source of the disease.

** heroic 〔hɪˈroˑɪk〕 *adj.* 勇敢的　　contribute 〔kənˈtrɪbjʊt〕 *v.* 貢獻
yellow fever 黃熱病　　civilian 〔səˈvɪljən〕 *adj.* 平民的
Cuba 〔ˈkjubə〕 *n.* 古巴　　major 〔ˈmedʒɚ〕 *n.* 少校
conduct 〔kənˈdʌkt〕 *v.* 指導　　isolate 〔ˈaɪsḷˌet〕 *v.* 隔離
rule out 排除　　sanitation 〔ˌsænəˈteʃən〕 *n.* 衛生

❖ Comprehension ❖

1. What was ruled out by previous tests?
   - (A) sanitary conditions
   - (B) mosquitoes
   - (C) related diseases
   - (D) victims of the disease

2. You are likely to take yellow fever when you _____.
   - (A) touch dirty areas
   - (B) eat contaminated food
   - (C) drink polluted water
   - (D) suffer a mosquito bite

3. Which of the following was a carrier?
   - (A) the volunteer
   - (B) the disease
   - (C) the insect
   - (D) the experiment

4. Clara Louise Maass was _____.
   - (A) a doctor
   - (B) an army major
   - (C) a nurse
   - (D) a Cuban citizen

** **mosquito** 〔məˈskito〕 *n.* 蚊子
   carrier 〔ˈkærɪə〕 *n.* 傳染媒介
   contract 〔kənˈtrækt〕 *v.* 染患
   participate 〔pəˈtɪsəpet〕 *v.* 參與
   conclusive 〔kənˈklusɪv〕 *adj.* 確定的
   contaminated 〔kənˈtɛmə‚netɪd〕 *adj.* 汚染的

   suspect 〔səˈspɛkt〕 *v.* 懷疑
   insect 〔ˈɪnsɛkt〕 *n.* 昆蟲

71 The Disco-Dancing Parliamentarian

ROME（Reuters）— Italy's Deputy Prime Minister, Gianni de Michelis, has some strong advice for politicians and businessmen suffering from stress — go disco dancing.

" Everybody needs to relax, managers, teachers, politicians....Some people have golf, but I believe in dancing," the minister told journalists last week.

He demonstrated his technique at his favorite resort on Italy's east coast recently. Showing extraordinary stamina, which his aides ascribe to practice, the minister danced until 6 a.m., spinning and clapping to the loud rhythm in two dance clubs, then dozed on his official plane before attending a Rome cabinet meeting at 11. To combat _____ , De Michelis recommends "doses" of up to an hour of dancing twice a week. "We politicians have our heads so full of things we need to relax, so we should dance," he explains.

** **parliamentarian**〔͵pɑrləmen'terɪən〕*n.* 國會議員
Reuters〔'rɔɪtəz〕*n.* 路透社（英國的通訊社）
deputy〔'dɛpjətɪ〕*adj.* 副的　　*prime minister* 總理；首相
stress〔strɛs〕*n.* 緊張　　**journalist**〔'dʒɜnlɪst〕*n.* 記者

◈ Comprehension ◈

1. What word fits in the blank?
   (A) stress　　　　　(B) enemies
   (C) illness　　　　　(D) dancing

2. The article presents _____.
   (A) a politician's advice on national problems
   (B) a dancer's advice on political problems
   (C) traditional Italian attitudes
   (D) a way to relax and relieve stress

3. Politicians _____.
   (A) are typically excellent dancers
   (B) don't have time for relaxation during the day
   (C) are more relaxed than teachers or managers
   (D) usually have extraordinary stamina

4. For Gianni de Michelis, dancing is _____.
   (A) a form of relaxation and exercise
   (B) a way of making friends
   (C) a cause of some stress
   (D) not popular among ordinary Italians

** **demonstrate** 〔'dɛmən,stret〕 *v.* 證明
resort 〔rɪ'zɔrt〕 *n.* 度假勝地　　**stamina** 〔'stæmənə〕 *n.* 精力
aide 〔ed〕 *n.* 助手　　*ascribe to* 歸因於　　**spin** 〔spɪn〕 *v.* 旋轉
clap 〔klæp〕 *v.* 拍手　　**rhythm** 〔'rɪðəm〕 *n.* 節拍
doze 〔doz〕 *v.* 打瞌睡　　**cabinet** 〔'kæbənɪt〕 *n.* 內閣
combat 〔kəm'bæt〕 *v.* 對抗　　**recommend** 〔,rɛkə'mɛnd〕 *v.* 推薦
dose 〔dos〕 *n.* 一劑藥

Irrational Fears

Suppose a child, playing in the attic, gets himself locked in a cedar chest from which he is unable to escape. He calls out in terror for help, but no one hears him and he remains imprisoned in the narrow darkness until he is missed some hours later at mealtime.

Twenty years later he may have forgotten about the chest and the hours he spent in it, yet when he finds himself in a telephone booth, a dark clothes closet, or a train berth, he may be overcome with an unnamed terror which is no less real and overpowering because it is to him unreasonable and unaccountable. The emotional system has a way of remembering things we have forgotten.

** **irrational** 〔ɪˊræʃənḷ〕 *adj.* 非理性的 **suppose** 〔səˊpoz〕 *v.* 假定
attic 〔ˊætɪk〕 *n.* 閣樓 **cedar** 〔ˊsidɚ〕 *n.* 西洋杉
chest 〔tʃɛst〕 *n.* 有蓋的大木箱 ***call out*** 大聲叫喊或呼救
imprison 〔ɪmˊprɪzn̩〕 *v.* 監禁 **miss** 〔mɪs〕 *v.* 注意到～的不在
booth 〔buθ, buð〕 *n.*（公用電話）亭 **berth** 〔bɝθ〕 *n.* 臥舖
be overcome with 因～而軟弱無力 **unnamed** 〔ʌnˊnemd〕 *adj.* 無名的
overpowering 〔͵ovɚˊpaʊərɪŋ〕 *adj.* 強烈的
unaccountable 〔͵ʌnəˊkaʊntəbḷ〕 *adj.* 無法解釋的

❖ Comprehension ❖

1. In the example, how long does the child remain in the chest?

   (A) one hour
   (B) a few hours
   (C) a few days
   (D) twenty years

2. According to this paragraph, a man may experience great fear because_____.

   (A) he has forgotten an important appointment
   (B) of an event which he has forgotten
   (C) of an unreasonable situation
   (D) he was once in prison

3. The person in the example might feel fear in all of the following EXCEPT_____.

   (A) telephone booth
   (B) dark closet
   (C) train berth
   (D) outdoors

4. According to this passage, which statement is true?

   (A) A man can overcome his fears if they are unreasonable.
   (B) A man may experience fear but not remember the reason.
   (C) Fear is always explainable.
   (D) Some fears are not real.

73 Modern Attitudes Toward Marriage

What modern couples are afraid of is commitment, both to each other and to an institution.

Commitment has a different meaning to the marriage-minded of the '80s, says Rachel Hare-Mustin, a professor of counseling and human relations at Villanova University. " Commitment means we'll stay together as long as we both want to, rather than *until death do us part*, " she says.

Yet, says a marriage counselor, " The only way to survive a marriage is to immerse yourself in it. Marriage doesn't work unless you see it as permanent. The whole thing becomes a little flat."

Unfortunately, couples today just don't trust marriage, he says. And *they get that from the statistics.*

** **commitment** 〔kə'mɪtmənt〕 *n.* 承諾
　　institution 〔,ɪnstə'tjuʃən〕 *n.* 機構　　**the marriage-minded** 想結婚的人
　　counseling 〔'kaʊnslɪŋ〕 *n.* 諮商　　**survive** 〔sə'vaɪv〕 *v.* 使繼續存在
　　immerse oneself in 投入於；埋首於
　　permanent 〔'pɜmənənt〕 *adj.* 永恆的　　**flat** 〔flæt〕 *adj.* 乏味的
　　statistics 〔stə'tɪstɪks〕 *n.* 統計

❖ Comprehension ❖

1. This passage states that modern couples expect to remain together_____.
   (A) as long as they want to
   (B) until one partner dies
   (C) because they are afraid
   (D) because they trust statistics

2. According to the marriage counselor, the only way to keep a marriage alive is to_____.
   (A) die
   (B) get counseling
   (C) listen to statistics
   (D) be committed

3. Modern couples mistrust marriage, because_____.
   (A) statistics show that many marriages fail
   (B) their marriages have become flat
   (C) they are immersed in their marriages
   (D) the economy has developed rapidly

4. Who are "the marriage-minded of the '80s"?
   (A) people in their 80s who want to get married
   (B) people who don't want to get married
   (C) marriage counselors and sociologists
   (D) people who want to get married

** mistrust 〔mɪs'trʌst〕 v. 不信；懷疑

sociologist 〔,soʃɪ'ɑlədʒɪst〕 n. 社會學家

74

Social Maturity

A socially mature person gets along well with all types of people in all types of situations. He does not necessarily like or respect all people, but he is tolerant and understanding and does not intentionally hurt anyone's feelings. Nor does he discriminate against people because of their race, religion, national origin, or their social and economic status.

The child and the adolescent often act as if they own their friends. The socially mature person does not demand the exclusive attention of his friends, nor does he show jealousy of their other friendships.

His affection, however, is strong and lasting because he does not become completely disillusioned when he sees a flaw in a friend's character. While he may prefer companionship to solitude, he can amuse himself and be happy when alone.

** **maturity** 〔mə'tʃʊrətɪ〕 *n.* 成熟　　*get along with* 相處
　not necessarily 未必；不一定　**tolerant** 〔'tɑlərənt〕 *adj.* 寬容的
　understanding 〔,ʌndə'stændɪŋ〕 *adj.* 能體諒別人的

◈ Comprehension ◈

1. According to the passage, socially mature people do not discriminate on the basis of their_____.

(A) sex   (B) political views
(C) sexual preference   (D) wealth

2. Socially mature people _____.

(A) prefer companionship to solitude
(B) demand the exclusive attention of friends
(C) intentionally hurt others
(D) become disillusiond by flaws in a friend's character

3. Which is not true of socially mature people?

(A) They get along with all types of people.
(B) They like and respect everyone.
(C) They are tolerant and understanding.
(D) Their affection is strong and lasting.

4. Who acts "as if they own their friends"?

(A) socially mature people   (B) jealous people
(C) foreigners   (D) adult companions

** **intentionally** 〔ɪn'tɛnʃənḷɪ〕 *adv.* 故意地
discriminate against 歧視   **adolescent** 〔,ædḷ'ɛsn̩t〕 *n.* 青少年
exclusive 〔ɪk'sklusɪv〕 *adj.* 獨佔的   **jealousy** 〔'dʒɛləsɪ〕 *n.* 嫉妒
affection 〔ə'fɛkʃən〕 *n.* 感情   **disillusion** 〔,dɪsɪ'luʒən〕 *v.* 幻滅
flaw 〔flɔ〕 *n.* 缺陷   **companionship** 〔kəm'pænjən,ʃɪp〕 *n.* 友誼
solitude 〔'salə,tjud〕 *n.* 孤獨

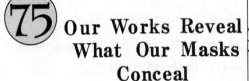75 Our Works Reveal What Our Masks Conceal

A man's work reveals him. In social intercourse he gives you the surface that he wishes the world to accept, and you can only gain a true knowledge of him by inferences from little actions, of which he is _____, and from fleeting expressions, which cross his face unknown to him. *Sometimes people carry to such perfection the mask they have assumed that* in due course they actually become the person they seem. But in his book or his picture the real man delivers himself defenceless. His pretentiousness will only expose his vacuity. No affectation of peculiarity can conceal a commonplace mind. To the acute observer no one can produce the most casual work without disclosing the innermost secrets of his soul.

** **reveal** 〔rɪ'vil〕 *v*. 透露　　**conceal** 〔kən'sil〕 *v*. 隱藏
social intercourse 社交　　**inference** 〔'ɪnfərəns〕 *n*. 推論
fleeting 〔'flitɪŋ〕 *adj*. 飛逝的　　**assume** 〔ə'sjum〕 *v*. 採取
in due course 在適當的時候　　**deliver** 〔dɪ'lɪvɚ〕 *v*. 表達
pretentiousness 〔prɪ'tɛnʃəsnɪs〕 *n*. 矯飾
expose 〔ɪk'spoz〕 *vt*. 揭露 (= *disclose*)
vacuity 〔və'kjuətɪ〕 *n*. 空洞；空虛

◈ Comprehension ◈

1. What word is most suitable for the blank?
   (A) proud
   (B) famous
   (C) aware
   (D) unconscious

2. According to the author, in social situations people
   _____.
   (A) accept the world easily
   (B) conceal their real natures
   (C) reveal their true qualities
   (D) like books and pictures

3. According to the passage, an artist's_____ holds
   no secrets.
   (A) face   (B) mind
   (C) soul   (D) work

4. By "work," the author seems to mean_____.
   (A) hard physical labor
   (B) money-making activity
   (C) creative products
   (D) social intercourse

** **affectation** 〔,æfɪk'teʃən〕 *n.* 矯飾
   peculiarity 〔pɪ,kjulɪ'ærətɪ〕 *n.* 特性
   commonplace 〔'kɑmən,ples〕 *adj.* 平凡的 **acute** 〔ə'kjut〕 *adj.* 敏銳的
   innermost 〔'ɪnəmost〕 *adj.* 最深處的

Dear Ann Landers

Controversy Over Breast-Feeding

Dear Ann Landers:

In August I read an article in a newspaper in North Platte, Neb., about a new city ordinance in Dubuque, Iowa. This ordinance, imposing a ban on breast-feeding in public places, outlawed exposing the nipple while breast-feeding.

What kind of sick mind sees eroticism in the natural and loving act of breast-feeding a baby? Whenever I see a woman breast-feeding her child, I see a mother demonstrating her love for her baby.

Furthermore, I can't understand all the fuss about women exposing their breasts at any time. Breasts are not sex organs. They are nothing more than fatty tissue containing milk-producing glands. —W.C.L.B.

Dear W.C.L.B.:

I agree with you that the sight of a woman breast-feeding her child is not erotic or offensive. However, there are some people with different ideas who are offended. So, it is best to avoid breast-feeding in public places if possible.

❖ Comprehension ❖

1. W.C.L.B. thinks that breast-feeding is _____.

   (A) unhealthy for both mothers and children

   (B) erotic and therefore offensive

   (C) a demonstration of love

   (D) to be avoided if possible

2. Ann Landers' answer indicates that she _____.

   (A) is not offended by breast-feeding

   (B) thinks W.C.L.B.'s attitude is totally wrong

   (C) has no children herself

   (D) lives in Dubuque, Iowa

3. Ann Landers thinks women should avoid breast-feeding in public places _____.

   (A) because some people are offended

   (B) if they visit Dubuque, Iowa

   (C) because breast-feeding is an erotic act

   (D) unless they expose their nipples

** controversy〔'kɑntrə,vɝsɪ〕*n.* 爭論
   breast-feeding〔'brɛst,fidɪŋ〕*n.* 餵奶;哺乳
   Neb. = Nebraska 內布拉斯加(美國中部的一州)
   ordinance〔'ɔrdn̩əns〕*n.* 法令　impose〔ɪm'poz〕*v.* 強加
   ban〔bæn〕*n.* 禁令　outlaw〔'aʊt,lɔ〕*vt.* 使成爲非法
   expose〔ɪk'spoz〕*vt.* 使暴露　nipple〔'nɪpl̩〕*n.* 乳頭
   eroticism〔ɪ'rɑtə,sɪzm̩〕*n.* 色情
   demonstrate〔'dɛmən,stret〕*v.* 表露　fuss〔fʌs〕*n.* 大驚小怪
   fatty tissue 脂肪組織　gland〔glænd〕*n.* 腺
   offensive〔ə'fɛnsɪv〕*adj.* 無禮的
   indicate〔'ɪndə,ket〕*v.* 指出;顯示　totally〔'totəlɪ〕*adv.* 完全地

內文翻譯・習題解答

The Shopping List
購物單

　　布萊克太太的皮膚有點問題，所以她去找醫生治療，醫生叫她去當地的醫院做一些檢驗。第二天早上，醫生打電話給布萊克太太，告訴她一些該忌口的東西，因為這些東西可能是導致她皮膚病的原因。布萊克太太很仔細地把這些東西寫在一張紙上，然後她把這張紙放在電話旁邊，就出門去參加婦女聚會了。

　　兩個小時之後她回到家，發現先生正在等她。「哈囉，親愛的，」她先生說：「你要買的東西，我都幫你買了。」「你都幫我買了？」她吃驚地問：「你怎麼知道我要買什麼？」「我在電話旁邊看到你的購物單啊，」她先生答道。當然，布萊克太太只好告訴她先生，他買的這些東西，都是醫生不讓她吃的東西。

解答➡ 1.（C）　2.（B）　3.（A）　4.（D）

The Fight
打架

　　深夜裏，有兩個人在街上打架，把納斯瑞丁給吵醒了。納斯瑞丁生平最愛看人打架，於是他打開窗戶，探頭出去看。那兩個人發現納斯瑞丁在看他們，就跑到屋子的轉角處去打，納斯瑞丁不想錯過任何精彩片段，可是外頭又很冷，所以他包了一條毯子，才跑出去。

　　那兩個人還在相互叫罵和搏鬥，納斯瑞丁又更靠近一點，可是當他一走到那兩個人伸手可及的距離時，他們就把他的毯子給搶走了。納斯瑞丁太老了，根本追不上他們，於是只好哀聲嘆氣地回家睡覺。

　　「那兩個人為什麼要打架？」他太太問道。

「他們似乎是爲了我的毯子在打架，」納斯瑞丁回答：「因爲他們一拿到毯子，就不吵了！」

解答➡ 1.（B） 2.（B） 3.（C） 4.（A）

Don't Put All Your Eggs in One Basket
別把蛋放在同一個籃子裏

我的一位朋友有一次發現，我把紙鈔隨意地放在各個口袋中，結果有許多散落在胸前口袋內的信件和其他文件中，於是他對我說：「你對錢毫無概念，不懂得如何來保存它。」並且在我出國前夕，送我一個皮夾子。我把所有的紙鈔都放入那只皮夾中，同時覺得自己總算是個講求實際的人了。不幸的是，在短短一週內，有個更切實際的扒手偷走了那個皮夾，奪走了大筆金錢，這筆錢比起我以往不切實際時，任何一名扒手所能偷走的，要超出許多。

解答➡ 1.（B） 2.（C） 3.（B） 4.（D）

Ignorance Is Bliss
無知便是福

視覺敏銳的母雞，顯然要比近視眼的母雞境遇好，因爲視力好總強過視力差。但這不見得是一成不變的。

如果把穀物放在鐵絲網的一邊，而把母雞放在另外一邊，視覺敏銳的母雞立刻就會看到穀物，於是衝上前去，但是被鐵絲網擋住了；然而穀物近在眼前，又似乎不斷地對牠招手，結果牠會把所有的時間花在設法穿過鐵絲網上。

解答➡ 1.（C） 2.（C） 3.（D） 4.（D）

5 A Clever Solution
聰明的解釋

　　一家小建築公司的經理，接到一張購買兩隻白老鼠的帳單時，感到非常驚訝，這是他的一名工人買的。他問那名工人，為什麼要把帳單送到公司來。

　　工人答道：「您還記得我們整修的房子吧？我們必須將一些新的線路穿過長三十呎、寬約一吋的管子，這根管子裏有四個大彎道。大家都束手無策，結果我想到一個好辦法。我去買了兩隻白老鼠，一隻公的、一隻母的，然後把一根線綁在公老鼠身上，而比爾則在另一端抓著母老鼠；公老鼠一聽到母老鼠吱吱叫，就順著管子，衝去救她；當他穿過管子時，身後拖著線。這樣，我們就輕而易舉地將線的一端，綁到電線上，而後將電線穿過管子。」

　　經理付了兩隻白老鼠的帳單。

解答➡ 1.（D）　2.（A）　3.（C）　4.（C）

6 The Measure of Success
成功的標準

　　美國人以工作勤奮為傲，但是當他們整個週末都坐著無所事事時，也同樣引以為傲。

　　事實上，有些美國人是以假期的長短和次數，來衡量成功與否的。一年可以休假一個月的人，自認為比一年只有兩週假期的人，來得成功；許多人當老師，只因為老師一年有三個月的假期。

　　簡單地說，有些美國人認為，工作時間越少，就越成功。

解答➡ 1.（B）　2.（C）　3.（C）　4.（C）

7 A Truthful Letter
一封實話實說的信

十六歲的馬修‧霍伯斯已經在同一所學校唸了五年，而且表現一直很差。他很懶散，跟同學打架，對老師無禮，又不遵守校規；校長想盡各種方法，想讓他努力用功、行為檢點，但是這些功夫都白費了──最糟的是，隨著馬修年歲的增長，他把其他學弟都帶壞了。

最後，馬修還是畢業了，他到一家大公司去求職，公司的經理寫信給校長，想知道他對馬修的看法如何。校長很想實話實說，但是又不願意太尖酸刻薄，所以他在信上寫道：「如果你能讓馬修‧霍伯斯替你工作，你的運氣實在是太好了。」

解答 ➡ 1.（B） 2.（D） 3.（A） 4.（B）

8 A Trick That Backfired
聰明反被聰明誤

有位農夫在村子裏真是小氣得出了名。某天他說：「任何人只要願意幫我做一天工，我就供應他三餐，再給他二十五辨士。」一個飢餓的流浪漢接受了這項條件，只不過他對那三頓飯的興趣，遠大過錢。「你可以先吃早餐，」農夫說道：「然後再去工作。」農夫給他一份很少量的早餐之後又說：「你可以吃午餐了，這樣比較節省時間。」流浪漢同意了，又吃了很差勁的一頓午餐。然後農夫又開口說：「既然你正在吃東西，何不連晚飯也一起吃了？」

流浪漢吃完晚飯之後，農夫很高興地對他說：「現在你可以幹一整天的活了。」「很抱歉，」流浪漢在起身離去之前說：「我從來不在吃完晚飯之後工作。」

解答 ➡ 1.（B） 2.（A） 3.（D） 4.（C）

9 An Easy Choice
必然的選擇

　　有一天，某大海港的海軍警局，接到城裏酒吧打來的緊急電話。侍者說有一個體形壯碩的水手喝醉了，正在破壞酒吧裏的設備。當天晚上負責看守警局的海軍上士，說他立刻就趕過去。通常，海軍士官要去應付喝得爛醉如泥的水手時，都會挑選身材最壯的警員同行。但是這位士官很特別，他並不這麼做，反而挑選一位看起來最矮、最弱的人陪他到酒吧去，並且把鬧事的水手給逮捕了。

　　另外一位海軍上士問他：「你爲什麼不挑一個塊頭大一點的同行呢？你可能得跟喝醉酒的水手打架呢。」「沒錯，你說的很對，」負責看守的士官答道：「可是如果你看見兩個警察來逮捕你，其中一個身材跟另外一個根本不成比例，你會先對哪一個下手？」

解答➡ 1.（B）　 2.（A）　 3.（A）　 4.（D）

10 The Merry Widows
快樂的寡婦

　　布朗先生去戲院看戲，他發現四周有一群美國女士，有些是中年婦女，有一些則年紀相當大了。在戲院的布幕尚未拉起之前，她們一直在說話和開玩笑。

　　在第一幕戲演完之後，其中一位女士因爲同伴太吵了，而向布朗先生道歉。他告訴這位女士，他很高興看到這些美國女士，在英國玩得這麼愉快；布朗先生鄰座的這位女士，就告訴他這群婦女在英國的各項活動。

　　「你知道嗎？這些人我已經認識一輩子了，」她說：「她們的先生都去世了，所以她們自稱爲『快樂的寡婦』。她們在每年的夏天，都要出國一、兩個月，好好地玩一玩。我一直很想加入這個團體，可是一直到今年春天，我才具備入會的資格。」

解答➡ 1.（C）　 2.（A）　 3.（C）　 4.（C）

Flashes of Insight
靈機一動

　　想到好點子所帶給人的滿足感，是大多數的經驗所無法比擬的。

　　你有個問題要解決；你想了又想，直到你想累了，甚至把它忘了；或是你暫時把它擱在一邊，上床睡覺，但這時卻靈機一動！當你不去想它的時候，點子卻突然浮現在你的腦中，就像上天賜予的禮物一樣。這時你會高興不已，渾身舒暢。這個點子或許並不正確，但至少你可以嘗試一下。

　　當然，並非所有的點子，都是這樣想出來的；但有趣的是，很多點子都是靈機一動之下的產品，特別是那些最重要的點子。它們都是突如其來，並且燃燒著創造力的火焰。

解答➡ 1.（B）　2.（D）　3.（C）　4.（B）

A Slow Learner
學習遲鈍

　　在暑假一開始的時候，我就說服舅舅讓我買一輛腳踏車，可是舅媽卻反對，她說買了車之後，我只會把自己的脖子給扭斷；但是在我的堅持之下，舅媽還是同意了。所以在學校停課之前，我就訂購了一輛腳踏車，幾天之後，我就擁有一輛漂亮、全新的腳踏車。

　　我決定要自己學會騎車，學校裏的同學告訴我，他們在半小時之內就學會了。可是我一試再試，最後只得到一個結論：我實在不是普通的笨。我讓園丁扶著我的車後面，這已經夠傷人自尊了，可是儘管如此，在第一天早上結束的時候，我還是跟一開始時一樣，沒有辦法自己騎上去。

解答➡ 1.（B）　2.（B）　3.（B）　4.（A）

A Man in a Hurry
趕時間的人

　　小鎮的警官，在大街上攔住一個超速駕駛的人，「可是，警官，」那人開口說：「我可以解釋——」

　　「閉嘴，」警官吼道：「我要把你送去拘留所冷靜冷靜，等候局長回來。」

「可是，警官，我只是想說——」

「我叫你閉嘴，你準備進拘留所吧！」幾個小時之後，警官進來看他的犯人，並說道：「算你走運，局長去參加他女兒的婚禮了，等他回來之後，心情一定不錯。」

「算了吧，」囚房裏的人答道：「因爲新郎就是我。」

解答 ➡ 1.（D）　2.（A）　3.（B）　4.（C）

14 World War Ⅳ
第四次世界大戰

在第二次世界大戰剛結束時，流傳著一個令人毛骨悚然的笑話。這個笑話是說，原子彈是下一次世界大戰最主要的武器，而弓箭則是再下一次世界大戰最重要的武器。

這個笑話很貼切地說明一個事實：戰爭這種災難，可以把我們科技上所有相互依賴的特徵摧毀殆盡，如果我們想從金字塔的底端再造這一切，得再花上數世紀的時間。

解答 ➡ 1.（C）　2.（B）　3.（B）　4.（B）

15 A Survivor
生存者

在三億六千萬年以前，大螃蟹就存在了，而且外表看起來跟今天差不多。牠是從史前時代一直到現在，外貌還保持不變的少數生物之一。蟑螂和印度洋的一種稀有魚類，是僅存的兩種年代與大螃蟹一樣古老的生物。當地球還在形成，山嶽還在升起的時候，大螃蟹就已經在海裏游動了。大螃蟹的肉並不可口，對抗牠們的天敵也不多，所以很占優勢，可能會再生存幾百萬年之久。

解答 ➡ 1.（C）　2.（C）　3.（C）　4.（D）

Dear Ann Landers / Unfair Interference
不公平的干涉

親愛的安‧蘭德絲：

我是個十六歲的女孩。去年夏天，我們全家去度假時，我認識了一群和我年紀相仿的朋友，他們不抽煙，也不喝酒，都是規矩、純潔的年輕人。其中有一個十八歲的男孩很喜歡我；而從那時候開始，我們就一直保持連繫。上個星期，艾廸寫信告訴我，他已經存夠了錢，打算來看我，他說他在城裏有個朋友，他要住在那個朋友家裡。我非常興奮，就跑去告訴父母。

昨天媽的舉止很奇怪，我馬上知道有什麼事不對勁了。我終於使她說出實情。原來她拍了一封電報給艾廸，要他取消行程，因為我「不太想」和他見面，而且簽的是我的名字。

我好難過。艾廸只是一個朋友，又不是情人。媽說她是為我好，因為艾廸的年齡太大，不適合我。我想聽聽妳的意見。

　　　　　　　　　　　　　　　　　——受到不平對待的人

親愛的U.T.：

妳的署名就是我的意見。妳母親應該先把她的不滿告訴妳，然後妳們再一起討論，看怎樣做最好。

解答➡ 1.（D） 2.（D） 3.（A）

16 An April Fool's Trick
愚人節的花招

有些國家的人們，喜歡在四月一日這天，想辦法開別人的玩笑。如果他們開的玩笑成功了，就會笑著說：「四月的笨蛋！」

在四月一日那天，有一輛鄉間巴士，在蜿蜒的公路上行駛的時候，速度突然減慢，最後停了下來。司機轉過身來對乘客說：「這輛公車太老舊了，現在只有一個辦法，我數到三之後，希望你們每一個人都往前傾，這樣應該可以使公車重新發動。好，現在請儘量把身子往後傾，預備好。」乘客全都向後傾，把背緊靠在椅子上，迫不及待地等著。

司機數：「一！二！三！」乘客們全都很快地往前一擺——巴士快速地起動了。

乘客們臉上都露出欣慰的微笑，但是當司機高興地大叫：「四月的笨蛋」時，他們的微笑先是轉變成驚訝的呼聲，然後變成歡愉的大笑。

解答➡ 1.（B）　2.（B）　3.（D）　4.（B）

 ## Smoking Patterns of Teenagers
青少年的抽煙模式

青少年的抽煙模式，在許多方面都跟成年人類似。社會經濟背景較好的青少年，以及在高中修大學預備課程的青少年，抽煙的比例比較小。

對青少年抽煙影響極大的一個因素，是家庭的抽煙習慣。如果父母親之一或二者都抽煙，或是哥哥姐姐抽煙，那麼青少年就比較容易開始抽煙；如果雙親之中有一個或者二個都不住在家裏，那麼青少年抽煙的可能性也比較大。

解答➡ 1.（C）　2.（B）　3.（B）　4.（B）

 ## Economy ── Not Always the Best Policy
節儉並非上策

在預算很緊的情況下，我請我太太替我剪頭髮，她同意了，但卻提醒我，她從未接受過專業訓練。一小時後，在她的利剪下，我的頭活像是頂了個茅草屋頂。

仍舊為了省下幾毛錢，我跑到當地的理髮學院去，看看是否能有所改善。我坐下來之後，學生突然說他有事情要走開一會兒，過了不久，他和他的老師一塊兒回來。「他來的時候，就是這副德性，」學生說：「真的！我還沒碰過他哩！」

解答➡ 1.（C）　2.（B）　3.（B）　4.（C）

19 A Practical Student
重實際的學生

這是一則住在肯塔基州小男孩的故事。有一次試卷中問道:「如果你去店裏買六分錢的糖果,給店員十分,店員該找你多少?」小男孩回答:「我從不曾有過十分錢,就算我有這些錢,也不會把它花在糖果上頭,因為無論如何,家裏的糖果都是媽媽做的。」主試者再出一道題目:「如果你替父親放牧十隻母牛,其中六隻走失了,趕回家的有幾隻?」小男孩答道:「我們家沒有十隻母牛,就算真的有十隻牛,如果我遺失了六隻,一定不敢回家了。」主試者仍不氣餒,又出了一道題目:「如果學校有十個小孩,其中六個得了麻疹,學校還剩下幾個學生?」答案是:「一個也沒有,因為其他的小孩也害怕得到麻疹。」

解答➡ 1.(A) 2.(D) 3.(A) 4.(B)

20 A Hesitant General
猶豫不決的將軍

在美國南北戰爭期間,亞伯拉罕・林肯的問題很嚴重──北方沒有訓練有素的軍隊,也沒有好的將領。在戰爭的頭一、兩年,北軍的總司令頻頻換人,喬治・麥克萊倫就是早期的將領之一。

麥克萊倫是一位好將軍,但他也是一個非常仔細的人;他似乎太過仔細了,以致無法成為一流的將軍。在進攻之前,他總是等了又等,準備又準備。每個人,包括林肯在內,都對他失去耐心。最後林肯寫一封信給他,信裏說道:

「親愛的麥克萊倫:如果你不想使用軍隊,我想跟你借用一下。

亞伯拉罕・林肯 敬上」

解答➡ 1.(B) 2.(B) 3.(C) 4.(B)

A Wise Grandmother
聰明的祖母

　　經過母親家順道拜訪時，我發現哥哥跟他的兩個小孩也在那裏。吉姆的兩個兒子，一個七歲、一個九歲，很快就在房子裏跑來跑去，使勁地帶上門，非常惹人厭。

　　當他們的喧嘩聲到達極點時，吉姆很嚴厲地指責他們。然而，母親馬上就護著這兩個小孩，她告訴吉姆別對他們太嚴厲。「媽！」吉姆吼道：「他們是我的小孩，我有百分之百的權力來糾正他們。」

　　母親微笑並柔聲地說：「吉姆，我很高興我們的看法一致，我也在糾正我的小孩。」

解答➡ 1.（C）　2.（A）　3.（A）　4.（D）

Valuable Salt
珍貴的鹽

　　大部份的人每天都用鹽。我們用鹽來使食物變得更好吃。我們覺得鹽一直都存在，沒什麼了不起，所以也就理所當然地使用。但是，曾經有一度，鹽並沒有那麼普遍。

　　在古代，鹽是奢侈品，只有富人才能用。希臘故事中提到，住在內陸的人，食物中是不加鹽的。鹽還曾經因為太難取得，而被當做錢來使用。有一段時間，羅馬工人的全部或部份工資，還是用鹽來支付的呢！所以我們有「比他的鹽還不值」這種說法。英文中" salary "（薪水）的來源是拉丁文的" salarium "，也就是「以鹽當錢」的意思。

解答➡ 1.（B）　2.（A）　3.（C）　4.（D）

Alienation and Aging
疏遠與老化

　　一個人的年紀越大，就越沈默。

　　年輕人總想向全世界傾吐自己的心聲；他們認為人與人之間，有一種深切的友誼，因此想投入他人的懷裏，而且相信別人也一定會接納自己；

他們想完全敞開自己，好讓別人瞭解自己，同時也想瞭解別人；他們的生命彷彿滿得溢出來，而和他人的生命交滙在一起，就像萬流歸宗於海一樣。

但是這種活力會漸漸消失，一道壁壘會聳立在自己與他人之間，這時人們才領悟到，他人與自己眞是形同陌路。

—— 毛姆

解答 ➡ 1.（A） 2.（A） 3.（D） 4.（C）

24 A Terrifying Moment
可怕的時刻

廸克發現自己必須同時做兩份工作，才能賺到足夠的錢來付學費。

有一年夏天，廸克設法白天在肉店工作，晚上則到醫院上班。在肉店裏，肉商通常讓廸克去招呼客人，自己則到另一個房間去算帳。另一方面，在醫院他當然只能做一些最簡單的工作，例如幫忙把病人從醫院的某處送到另一處去。廸克在肉店及醫院裏，都必須穿上白色的衣服。

某晚在醫院裏，廸克要幫忙把一位女士從病房送到動手術的地方。這位女士本來就已經很害怕了，在見了廸克之後，簡直是要她的命。她大叫：「不要！不要！不要屠夫，我不要屠夫替我動手術。」然後就暈過去了。

解答 ➡ 1.（C） 2.（C） 3.（A） 4.（D）

25 Not That Kind of Painter！
是畫家，不是油漆匠！

一位生活僅夠糊口的年輕藝術家，和他的妻子一同參加宴會，有一位客人問他如何謀生，他回答：「我是一位畫家。」

「太棒了！」客人說道。「我家的牆壁想再油漆一次，我付你九百塊錢，來做這件差事。」

「可是你不瞭解，」藝術家說：「我是一位畫家，你知道嗎？就像米開蘭基羅一樣。」

「那是什麼意思？」客人問道。

藝術家的妻子插嘴說：「你剛才是說九百塊錢？」

「沒錯，」客人回答。

「米開蘭基羅的意思是，」她回答：「他很願意連你的天花板也一起油漆。」

解答➡ 1.（D）　2.（C）　3.（A）　4.（D）

The IRS Strikes Again
國稅局的老把戲

　　小男孩的父親去世了，而守寡的母親入不敷出，於是小男孩就寫了一封信：

　　「親愛的天父：可不可以請祢寄一百元給我母親？她現在的生活實在是太艱苦了。」

　　這封信最後到了郵政總局。拆看這封信的職員深受感動，於是他存下幾塊錢，又把這封信拿給郵局其他的職員看，總共募集了五十元之後，把這些錢寄給小男孩。幾個星期以後，小男孩又寫信來了，這次是一封道謝的信，只不過他還指出，上帝經由華盛頓寄來這封信，實在不對，因為一如慣例，美國政府又扣掉了百分之五十的稅金。

解答➡ 1.（B）　2.（A）　3.（B）　4.（C）

Never Satisfied
毫不知足

　　一個小男孩和溺愛他的祖母，正沿著邁阿密海灘散步。忽然，天外飛來一個大浪，把這個小孩捲入海中。祖母嚇得趕忙跪下，舉頭望天，乞求上帝把她心愛的孫子還給她。

　　於是，看啊！又來了個大浪，把目瞪口呆的小孩抬起，然後在她面前的沙灘上把他放下。祖母仔細地將小孩檢查一遍之後，知道他平安無事。

不過，她還是生氣地望著天空。「我們來的時候，」她憤慨地尖叫著：「他戴了一頂帽子。」

解答➡ 1.（C）　2.（B）　3.（D）　4.（B）

A Playboy
花花公子

　　我們家對面住著一個退休的人，他常常坐在走廊上，看看鄰居在做些什麼。我白天是老師，因此穿着很保守；然而，在閒暇時，我積極參與戲劇工作，所以來來去去常穿戴各種不同的服裝及假髮。

　　某天下午，我先生把垃圾拿出去丟時，我們這位鄰居向他走過來。「你帶著那些女人進進出出，却不會被你太太發現，你究竟是怎麼辦到的？」他問。

　　我先生只是笑一笑，眨一眨眼。稍後，當我聽說這件事時，我問道：「你真的告訴他事實了嗎？」

　　「什麼！」我先生大叫：「我才不想英名掃地呢！」

解答➡ 1.（D）　2.（A）　3.（A）　4.（D）

A Man of Principle
有原則的人

　　我們全船的人開始捕鱈魚，並且捕獲很多。到當時為止，我一直堅決不吃葷食。在這件事上面，我同意我的老師崔昂的想法：捕捉魚類是一種缺乏正當理由的謀殺，因為魚類不曾、也不會對我們造成什麼傷害，所以這種屠殺就名不正、言不順。這種想法似乎非常合理；但我從前是很喜歡吃魚的，尤其當魚從煎鍋中熱騰騰地端出來時，聞起來真是棒極了。我在原則和愛好間猶豫了好一陣子，後來我想起：當魚被剖開時，我看見牠們的肚子裏有更小的魚，於是我想：「如果你們能彼此殘殺，我不懂為什麼我們不能吃你們？」因此，我痛快地吃了一頓鱈魚大餐。

　　　　　　　　　　　　——摘自班傑明・富蘭克林自傳

解答➡ 1.（A）　2.（C）　3.（C）　4.（C）

30 The Vital Role of Risk
冒險的重要性

冒險是心靈的必備糧食。

缺乏冒險會令人產生一種厭倦，這種厭倦麻痺人心的方式，雖然與恐懼不同，程度卻是一樣的。冒險是一種會引起理性反應的危險，換句話說，它不會讓你的心智無計可施，而嚇得崩潰。

人類想保護自己免於害怕與恐懼，但這並不意味著可以免除冒險；相反地，這表示人們在社交生活的每一個層面中，永遠都要有相當程度的冒險精神。因為缺乏冒險，會使人的勇氣減弱，甚至消失殆盡，一旦有急難發生，內心對恐懼必然毫無招架之力。在這種情況下，我們該做的就是讓冒險精神挺身而出，而不至於轉變成致命感。

解答➡ 1.（C）　2.（B）　3.（C）　4.（B）

分析➡ <u>leaving</u> <u>the soul</u>, *if the need should arise*, <u>without the</u>
　　　　　V　　　O　　　　　　　　　　　　　　　　OC

<u>～ fear.</u> 「一旦有急難發生，內心對恐懼必然毫無～。」

Dear Abby / Gratitude
感恩

親愛的艾比：

許多年前的一個早上，我姨媽冒著風雪，吃力地到田園裡的信箱去拿信；她打開信箱，發現裡面有一隻黑白相間的小土狗，奄奄一息，幾乎快凍僵了。她把那隻小傢伙帶進屋內，替牠取名東尼，並照顧牠，直到牠恢復健康。那時每個人都認為她瘋了。

二十年後，也是在一個飄雪的寒冷多夜，患關節炎又重聽的老東尼，把正在二樓房間裡熟睡的姨媽叫醒，並帶她逃到安全的地方；這時，整棟房子已經燒毀，並且倒塌在他們身旁。

當消防人員終於抵達時，剩下的只有壁爐和兩層樓高的煙囪，以及東尼和我姨媽！

這種感恩的行為，妳覺得如何？——瑪麗恩，拉斯維加斯親愛的瑪麗恩：

太感人了！有件事妳和其他讀者一定很樂於知道。根據我最近所收到的讀者來信，過去人們常以獵槍來結束流浪狗痛苦的情形，現在已經有了戲劇化的改變。越來越多的人願意設法照顧狗兒，使牠們恢復健康。

解答➡ 1.（C） 2.（C） 3.（C）

③1 Deciphering Faces
讀人們的臉

並非我以貌取人，而是人們的面孔令我著迷。我不會盯著別人看，我喜歡把某人臉部的印象帶回家，然後在私底下細細地看，好好地玩味，就像野獸喜歡在隱蔽處，吞食牠的獵物一樣。

如果以此來判斷一個人的性格，很容易產生誤解，但事實上，這個產生誤解的因素，正是使我滿足的主因。在讀一張臉，及其形狀、神采、線條的過程中（就好像這些都是傳遞內部訊息的文字、語句一樣），我賦與這張臉一個性格，這是我深感興趣的事，雖然這個性格可能被扭曲，不完全錯誤，也不完全正確。我的猜測與事實間的距離，就如同杜撰與歷史之間的差距一樣。我不會替這個習慣辯白，但這卻是我所做的事情之一。

解答➡ 1.（C） 2.（B） 3.（C） 4.（C）

③2 Sex Discrimination
性別歧視

合眾國際社聖地牙哥報導——五名消防隊的女性受訓員全被退訓，其中四名是因為不夠強健，有一名則是因為受傷。

「體力是最主要的問題，」消防隊長李奧那‧貝爾，在星期二五名女士從消防學院退學後這麼說道。

「我們並不是說女性不能從事這項工作，我們只是說這幾位女士沒有體力來做這項工作，」他說。

在同時，這幾位女士召開記者招待會，說明她們可能聘請律師，控告聖地牙哥市性別歧視，並且正在尋求女權團體的支持。

以前是救生員，現年二十六歲的卡洛・泰勒抱怨說：「這個訓練根本就是用來淘汰女性的。」

解答➡ 1.（A） 2.（C） 3.（C） 4.（C）

33 Transmission of Culture
文化的薪傳

當小孩逐漸長大，四周都是兄弟姐妹、父母，甚至大家庭的成員時，他會逐漸學習到自己周遭社會的一些事情。換句話說，小孩最初是在與家人的接觸中，學習到社會文化。個人習得社會文化的方式，叫做「社會化」。社會化並不侷限於父母與子女間的溝通與關係，也並非在孩童時代就完成，而是終生都在進行。目前，社會科學家所做的研究指出，社會化的初期，對個人的發展極為重要，因為這個時期對一個人的想法和態度，有著深遠的影響。

解答➡ 1.（A） 2.（B） 3.（D） 4.（D）

34 The Greatest Regret
最深的懊悔

小時候，由於我總是不願意告訴父母，我是多麼喜歡他們為我做的事，所以一直無法帶給他們快樂。我不知道在我的生命中，還會有什麼比這件事更讓我深切悔恨的。

時至今日，我才了解到，我對他們替我所做的安排毫無反應，一定令他們一再地感到困惑、沮喪以及椎心的失望。例如，他們帶我去倫敦看法英博覽會，而我的表現是多麼令人心痛啊！當我應該表現出快樂的時候，我的心中總好像有個小惡魔在阻止著我。

解答➡ 1.（C） 2.（D） 3.（A） 4.（C）

35 Emotions：Express，Don't Repress
情緒要表達，不要壓抑

　　如果小孩子因為表現出憤怒而受到處罰，或是因為表現出恐懼而感到很羞恥，或是因為表達他的喜愛而遭受嘲弄，那麼他就會以為，表達真實的感情是「錯」的。

　　有些小孩會認為，只有表達「不好的情緒」，如憤怒和恐懼，才是罪惡或錯誤的；但是，在你抑制壞情緒的同時，你也遏止了好情緒的表達。評判情緒的標準，不在其本身的「好」與「壞」，而在於其適切與否。如果在小徑上遇見熊，那麼感到恐懼就很正當。如果有充份的理由，需要憑著具有毀滅性的力量，來消除一項障礙，這時感到憤怒則是再適切不過了。因為，只要加以適當的引導及控制，憤怒不啻為構成勇氣的重要因素。

解答➡ 1.（C）　2.（C）　3.（D）　4.（C）

36 Outwitted
青出於藍

　　「你們有整整兩個鐘頭的時間，」教授邊說邊把考卷發給全班學生。「時間到之後才交上來的考卷，我絕不收。」兩個小時之後，他打破教室的寂靜，說:「時間到。」但是有一個學生卻仍繼續奮力不懈地作答。

　　大約十五分鐘後，這個遲交的學生才把考卷抓在背後，向教授走過來。教授從整堆考卷後面瞪著他，並拒收他的考卷；於是他站直了身子問:「教授，你知道我是誰嗎？」

　　「不知道，」教授說。

　　「太好了，」學生一面回答，一面把他的考卷塞進整堆考卷中。

解答➡ 1.（B）　2.（A）　3.（B）　4.（B）

37 Changing Attitudes Toward Children
改變管敎小孩的態度

　　從前人們要求小孩子必須做到的絕對服從和尊敬，我們現在已經不太重視了。「溫順」或「很聽話」這類的字眼，在今天使用起來，批評的意味遠超過讚美。

　　一般認爲，父母的責任，在於證明自己值得小孩尊敬；要使小孩由衷生出敬意，而不能把尊敬當成天賦權利般，要求小孩做到。對於孩子而言，強調的重點也不再是服從和責任，而是信任與愛；不是謙卑，而是道德勇氣和獨立。養育小孩長大成人，也就是要訓練他，使他獨立。

解答➡ 1.（D）　　2.（C）　　3.（C）　　4.（B）

38 The Truth About Exercise
運動的眞義

　　生理學家一度相信，對四十歲以上的人而言，任何形式的運動都是有害的。但我們做醫生的也一樣難辭其咎，因爲我們總是警告四十歲以上的病人要「輕鬆一點」，並要他們放棄高爾夫球以及其他運動。二十年前，一位著名的作家，甚至建議四十歲以上的人，可以坐的時候，千萬不要站著，而可以躺下的時候，千萬不要坐著——他認爲這樣可以「保存」體力和能量。

　　然而，今天的生理學家及醫學博士，其中包括執全國牛耳的心臟專家，卻告訴我們，運動，甚至激烈的運動，不但可以做，而且對於任何年紀的人來說，都是保持健康不可或缺的一環。你絕不會老到不能運動的地步。

解答➡ 1.（D）　　2.（C）　　3.（B）　　4.（C）

39 Jumping to Conclusions
遽下斷語

　　我們每個人多多少少都會受限於自己的職業眼光。裁縫師只要上下打量一下你的穿著，就會根據你衣服的剪裁及光鮮程度，來給你打分數。做靴子的人只要對你的靴子瞟上一眼，他也會依據靴子的品質及使用情形，來衡量你的智商、社會地位及財務狀況。

牙醫也是如此。他用牙齒來評斷全世界。只要你張開嘴讓他瞧瞧，他對你的人格、習慣、健康狀況、身份，和心性，就會建立起堅定不移的看法。

解答➡ 1.（C） 2.（D） 3.（C） 4.（A）

 ## Two Views of Marriage
對婚姻的兩種看法

她正在給兒子寫信，祝賀他訂婚。

「我親愛的兒子，」母親寫著：「這消息眞是太棒了！你父親和我都因爲你找到幸福而高興不已。我們向來最大的心願，就是希望你能娶到一個好女人。好女人是上天賜給男人最珍貴的禮物。她可以把男人的優點全部激發出來，還可以幫他壓制住所有的邪惡。」

接著是個不同筆跡所寫的附筆。

「你媽拿郵票去了。不要結婚啊，你這個傻小子！」

解答➡ 1.（A） 2.（B） 3.（D） 4.（A）

 ## An Unrecognized Vice
不爲人知的惡習

一個人可能過份沈溺於閱讀，正如他可能過份沈溺於其他美好的事物一樣。過度熱衷閱讀，反而會變成一種不良習慣——如果不能察覺這一點，這個不良習慣就更加危險。

但是，過度閱讀是唯一未受應得指責的自我放縱形式。這個事實很令人驚訝，因爲只要誠實地觀察自己與他人，任何人都會發現：過度閱讀消耗一個人的時間、浪費他的精力、破壞他的思考力，還會轉移他的注意力，使他脫離現實。

——選自奧爾德斯·赫胥黎，「適當的閱讀」

解答➡ 1.（B） 2.（B） 3.（A） 4.（D）

42 Appreciating Distance
珍惜距離

　　我認為父親沒有車，對我而言是一種福份，雖然我大部份的朋友都有車。想去那裏就衝出去，這種銳不可當的力量，我從來就不曾擁有過，我是以自身內燃器的標準來衡量距離的。我並不允許自己小看距離這個觀念，相反地，開車者心中的一小段距離，卻讓我擁有無數的財富。現代運輸最真實，也最恐怖的聲明是它「使距離消失」，它的確辦到了這一點，他消滅了上天賜予我們最神聖的一項贈與。這種不良的誇大，減低了距離的價值，以至於今天一個年輕人，就算遊歷了一百哩，心中那種解放、朝聖、冒險的感覺，會比他的祖父當年遊歷了十哩路，還來得少。

解答➡ 1.（B）　2.（D）　3.（A）　4.（A）

43 That's Perfect
太完美了

　　某齣戲有個場景，必須製造出很美的落日效果。但是導演是個很難取悅的人；他對這個場景，事先已經有了特定的看法。

　　戲院的電工，很努力地想製造出這場落日的效果。他們嘗試各式各樣燈光的安排與組合——紅燈、橘燈、黃燈、藍燈，燈光由上方、後方、前方、兩側打過來——但是導演怎麼也不滿意。後來導演突然間看到他夢寐以求的效果，「就是這樣！」他很興奮地對著後台的電工大叫，「就維持這個樣子！」「很抱歉，先生，」電工工頭答道：「我們沒有辦法！」「為什麼沒辦法？」導演很生氣地問道。「因為戲院著火了，先生，」電工工頭答道：「正因為著火才製造出你現在所看到的效果！」

解答➡ 1.（B）　2.（B）　3.（C）　4.（A）

The Danger of Sensationalism
煽情的危險

　　報紙跟讀者之間的關係，很像喊「狼來了」的男孩，與很快就學會不去理會他的人們之間的關係。報紙不斷地在每一則消息中，注入人為的刺激，最後大眾會瞭解這種把戲，而感到很厭倦。讀者看到一個很嚇人的標題時，心裏會想：「這不過是另一則新聞報導罷了。」偶爾也會有一則重要性超過以往一百倍的新聞出現，值得每個讀者立即去注意與思考，但是報紙已經無法顯示這種不尋常的重要性。因為報紙已經用慣了煽情的文字與標題，所以這些方法再也不具特殊的效力。

解答➡ 1.（B）　2.（C）　3.（D）　4.（C）

An Encouraging Prediction
激勵人心的預言

　　就整體而言，我的學校生活頗令我沮喪。除了在劍術方面，我贏得公立學校的冠軍之外，其他都乏善可陳。我的同學和學弟們，似乎在每一方面，都比我更能適應學校這個小世界的環境；他們在運動及課業兩方面，都比我優秀得多。在競賽一開始，就感到自己完全被超越，這種滋味實在不好受。可是當我向校長威爾頓先生告別，聽到他很有自信地預測我會成功時，實在令我感到非常驚訝。為此我永遠都感激他。

解答➡ 1.（C）　2.（D）　3.（A）　4.（C）

Dear Ann Landers 　　　　**Overcoming a Phobia**
　　　　　　　　　　　　　　　　克服恐懼症

親愛的安·蘭德絲：

　　我已經跟一個非常好的女孩訂婚，打算明年結婚。昨天晚上她跟我說，她希望我不介意開著燈睡覺，因為她從小就怕黑，而且似乎無法克服這種恐懼感。

　　我告訴她，恐懼都是心理造成的，而且以後有我在她身邊，實在沒什麼好怕的。

　　安，她已經不是十幾歲的少女，而是成年女子了，我該怎麼辦？開著燈我又睡不著；我曾經試過一次，結果整夜都醒著。請幫幫我吧！

——巴拿馬市

親愛的巴拿馬：

　　所有的恐懼都是心理造成的。你要做的，是想辦法消除這種恐懼。我建議用漸進的方式：首先，在衣櫥裏或走廊上留一盞燈，把門半開著；然後再進展到只留一盞微弱的夜燈。同時，你可以嘗試戴眼罩，這在大部份藥房都買的到。希望這樣對你有所幫助。

解答➡ 1.（C）　2.（A）　3.（D）

46 Legal Aid
法律援助

　　和許多律師一樣，我先生會在深夜接到電話，通常是被拘捕的人打來的。可是有一晚，打電話來的人是一位很激動的女士，而她背後還有男士咆哮的聲音傳過來。

　　「如果男人遺棄太太，」這位女士想知道：「太太可以得到房子和傢俱嗎？」我先生告訴她，他不在電話中，給人法律上的建議，然後叫她打電話去他的事務所約個時間。

　　那位女士聽他說完話之後，便大聲地回答：「哦！你是說太太還可以取得車子、船及儲蓄存款嗎？非常謝謝你。」然後她就得意洋洋地把電話掛斷。

解答➡ 1.（C）　2.（D）　3.（A）　4.（D）

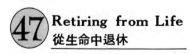

47 Retiring from Life
從生命中退休

　　許多人在退休之後，便很快地走向生命的下坡。他們覺得生命中有活力、有生產力的部份已經結束，工作也已經完成了。他們沒有任何期盼，從而變得厭煩、懶散；而且由於他們感到凡事都被摒除在外，自己也不再具有重要性，所以會失去自尊，痛苦不堪。他們會以看待沒有用處，毫無價值，而又疲憊不堪的寄生蟲那種眼光來看待自己。有不少人在退休一年左右就死亡了。

這些人之所以會死，並不是因為他們從工作崗位上退休，而是因為他們從生命中退休了。這是一種無用、完蛋的感覺，也是自尊、勇氣和自信的喪失。

解答 ➡ 1.（C）　2.（C）　3.（C）　4.（B）

48 How Italy Rediscovered Her Past
義大利的文藝復興

曾經有一段很長的時間，羅馬是文明的重心。但是，經過西元第四世紀哥德人和汪達爾人的侵略之後，羅馬帝國的勢力便告瓦解。然而，義大利人從未忘記他們國家輝煌的過去，並一直在設法恢復這種榮耀。

一四五三年，土耳其人佔領了君士坦丁堡，許多住在那兒，通曉希臘文的學者於是不得不往西逃。他們當中有不少人逃到義大利，並帶來古代的希臘文學作品；這些作品，在羅馬帝國敗亡後的數個世紀中，幾乎已經被西歐所遺忘。義大利人對這些學者的學識很感興趣，所以也就研究起古代藝術來了。簡單地說，這就是文藝復興發展的經過。

解答 ➡ 1.（D）　2.（C）　3.（A）　4.（B）

49 Speak Up !
大聲說出來 !

要養成說話比平時大聲的習慣。大家都知道，受到壓抑的人說話總是溫溫吞吞的。要把聲量提高。你不必對別人吼叫，也不必使用生氣的語調——你只要很自覺地練習，把話說得比平時大聲就可以了。大聲說話本身就可以有效地消除壓抑感。

　　最近有實驗證明，如果你在搬東西的時候，一面大叫或發出聲音，那麼你可以運用的力量，將會增加百分之十五，而搬得動的重量，也會增加。原因就在於大叫能消除壓抑感，並使你發揮出所有的力量，包括原來受到壓抑所阻礙而無法施展的力量。

解答➡ 1.（B）　2.（C）　3.（B）　4.（B）

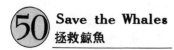

Save the Whales
拯救鯨魚

　　世界上有許多人，都為了海洋中鯨魚數目日漸減少，而憂心忡忡。人類約從十一世紀就開始捕鯨；有幾種鯨魚已經被獵殺過度了。最近，牠們的數目甚至已經減少到瀕臨絕種的邊緣。

　　人類為什麼要拯救鯨魚？原因在於鯨魚能幫助維持動植物間的平衡。人類已經破壞了這個平衡。人類製造的各種垃圾使得海洋中的鹽份增加；而增加的鹽份則有助於某些植物及小動物的生長。但是，這些動植物卻可能對魚類有害。鯨魚能夠大量地捕食這些在很鹹的海水中生長繁殖的動植物；所以，鯨魚非常重要，因為牠們維持著海洋環境的清潔，使魚類能悠游其中。

解答➡ 1.（C）　2.（D）　3.（D）　4.（A）

A Polite Request
客氣的要求

親愛的瓊斯先生：

　　近幾個星期以來，有一個問題愈來愈嚴重地困擾著內人和我，不知您是否能助我們一臂之力？大部份的夜晚，我們都過得很寧靜；但是，我們很不想告訴您，近來，大約從七點一直到半夜，我們常常聽見貴府收音機的聲音，比您所想的要大聲得多。不知您是否能將音量降低，尤其是在十點之後？我們都瞭解，由於我們的房子蓋得太近，所以偶爾有些不方便之處，也是無可厚非。不過，如果您能改善一下現況，那麼我們將會感激不盡，因為，最近我們經常睡眠不足。

羅伯特‧紐康 敬上

解答➡ 1.（A） 2.（A） 3.（A） 4.（C）

52 On Edge
如臨深淵

　　一位公司經理，帶著工作了一天的煩惱和「心情」回到家裏。一整天中，他倍受困擾，來去匆忙，還積極進取，並且要「隨時待命」。或許，他覺得有點受挫，致使他變得暴躁易怒。

　　當他回家時，他的身體是停止工作了；但是，他卻把剩餘的進取、挫折、匆忙和擔憂也帶了回家。他仍然處在隨時待命的狀態中，無法放鬆。他對妻子家人動輒發怒。雖然他對公司的問題束手無策，不過這些問題卻仍不斷地在他腦中盤旋。

解答➡ 1.（C） 2.（C） 3.（D） 4.（D）

53 Save the Sharks
拯救鯊魚

　　鯊魚危害人類的程度，還不及人類危害鯊魚的程度。雖然每年都有數百萬人大膽地往海裏跳，但是嚴重的鯊魚攻擊事件發生的比例，平均還不到五十件，而且其中只有十件置人於死地。這個比例之所以低，是因為大部份的鯊魚，都害怕像人類體積這麼大的動物。在我們所知道的三百五十種鯊魚當中，只有一種——大白鯊——是完全不怕人的。然而人類殘害鯊魚的數目卻是空前的，每年都有數以千計的鯊魚被獵殺，以作為食物，或者死於海裏用來保護游泳者的刺網。就連大白鯊的數量也不斷地減少，因為人們獵殺牠們，想取得牠們的牙齒和上下顎來賣給收藏家。或許人們應該少操心如何保護自己以抵抗鯊魚；而多想想如何保護鯊魚，以抵抗人類的殘害了。

解答➡ 1.（C）　2.（A）　3.（B）　4.（D）

The Mind as a Laboratory
頭腦實驗室

每當有人問愛因斯坦他的實驗室在哪裏,他就把鋼筆拿出來，說：「這就是了。」

如果他拍自己的頭，說同樣的話，或許更精確些；因為他在科學上最卓越的貢獻，並非物理實驗室裏的產品，而是他腦中思慮實驗下的結果。如果沒有這種思慮的實驗，他不大可能有這些洞察力，使人們在瞭解物質世界方面，有長足的進步。

解答➡ 1.（B）　2.（C）　3.（C）　4.（A）

Wake Them Up
叫醒他們

一位牧師把每當自己看到會衆在打瞌睡時，就派上用場的一個妙方，傳授給一位剛出道的牧師。「我會突然間告訴他們：『昨天晚上，我擁抱別人的老婆。』當每個人都吃驚地坐直身子的時候，我再補上一句：『那個女人就是我最親愛的母親。』」

年輕的牧師心想他可以依樣畫葫蘆。所以在接下來的那個星期天，當大部份的會衆都在打瞌睡的時候，他大聲地說：「你們知道嗎,？昨晚我擁抱別人的老婆。」吃驚的會衆馬上挺身坐直，盯著他看，這時牧師卻結結巴巴地說：「喔，我的天啊——我已經忘了她是誰了。」

解答➡ 1.（B）　2.（A）　3.（C）　4.（C）

A Hidden Cause of Accidents
意外事件的隱形肇因

　　保險公司以及其他研究意外事件起因的機構發現，情緒無法平息是許多汽車意外事件的肇因。如果駕駛人剛與太太或老板發生口角，或是前不久才遭遇挫折，或者剛離開他必須採取攻擊性行為的場合，發生意外的可能性會大得多。他把不適當的態度和情緒延伸到駕駛汽車上，而不是真的在生其他駕駛的氣。就像早晨由極度憤怒的夢裏醒來的人一樣，他知道加諸在他身上的不公平，只會在夢裏出現，但他還是非常生氣。

解答➡ 1.（C）　2.（C）　3.（A）　4.（C）

分析➡ He carries over into his driving attitudes and emotions
　　　　　S　　V　　　　　　　　　　　　　　　　O

　　　which are inappropriate.

　　「他把不適當的態度和情緒延伸到駕駛汽車上。」

Choosing a Resort
選擇度假地點

　　根據最近的一項調查顯示，大多數人對度假勝地的看法，都大同小異。

　　大眾運輸的便利與否，在選擇地點上無足輕重，即使對沒有車的人來說也是如此。根據調查，在受訪者中，有百分之四十認為，風景是決定假日去處最重要的因素。另外有百分之三十六的人，在選擇的時候，主要是受度假地點所提供的設備所影響。造訪朋友和天氣，則是其次考慮的要素。

解答➡ 1.（C）　2.（A）　3.（A）　4.（D）

Theater as Catharsis
劇場的淨化作用

　　一旦你進入劇場或戲院，就會把日常生活拋之腦後。當你一坐下，燈光一暗，就進入了另外一個世界。意志行為讓你暫時接受這個新世界是真實的。你承認在舞台上或螢幕中的人物眞的存在，他們的問題也是千眞萬確的。你看著故事一直發展下去，就會迷失了自我。你與其中某個角色合而爲一，他的失敗使你難過，他的成功使你喜悅，在這齣戲結束之前，你已經由衷地體驗了另外一個人的生活，以至於把自己的煩惱都拋到九霄雲外。當你再面對這些煩惱時，它們似乎已經有所不同。亞里斯多德把這種效果稱爲「淨化」。

解答➡ 1.（C） 2.（B） 3.（D） 4.（B）

Two National Characters
有其國必有其民

英國社會的一成不變，是貴族制度與習性之下，必然的結果。這使得英國人普遍比較內向，也比較不容易激動；他們的看法與嗜好比較穩定，也是基於同一個理由。英國人不輕易承諾，但是你可以信賴他們，因爲他們通常都會信守諾言。想結交一位英國朋友相當不容易，但是只要一日爲友，就終生爲友。

美國人的個性就比較親切、坦白、樂於助人，也比較容易結交朋友。美國人滿腔的熱情，使得他們承諾容易、守約難。由於他們比較容易激動，所以時常會被印象所矇騙，而這些印象經常都是轉瞬即逝的。

解答➡ 1.（B） 2.（A） 3.（B） 4.（C）

Reducing Anxiety
減少焦慮

如果我們瞭解，造成焦慮的事件是多麼微不足道的話，就可以減少很多焦慮。

我一生中發表過不少公開演講；剛開始的時候，我一看見聽衆就害怕，所以緊張得講也講不好。這種痛苦的考驗讓我怕得不得了，因此每次在演講之前，我都巴不得摔斷腿；而在演講過後，我又往往因爲神經過度緊張而疲憊不堪。

可是漸漸地，我告訴自己，講得好不好並不重要，因爲不管是好是壞，對世界一點影響也沒有。

我發現自己越不在乎演說的成敗，就講得越精彩，漸漸地，神經緊張幾乎已經消失無踪了。許許多多的神經疲乏，都可以如此應付。我們的所做所爲，並沒有自己想像中那麼重要；畢竟，我們的成功與失敗都不是舉足輕重的事。

解答➡ 1.（B） 2.（A） 3.（A） 4.（B）

Dear Ann Landers

A Pleasant Problem
令人愉快的難題

親愛的安·蘭德絲：

這封信不是在開玩笑。由於我長得很像保羅·紐曼，所以我的生命正走向毀滅之途。我現年三十歲，婚姻幸福，有三個小孩，而且按時上教堂做禮拜。但是我們這棟大樓的電梯小姐，經常會載我到地下室，按下「停止」的按鈕，然後想要對我示好。晚上我送保姆回家時，她也總是在道晚安時要我吻她。如果我找個小餐廳想吃頓便餐，就會有婦女圍過來要我簽名。昨天，我太太看見我和一個漂亮的年輕小姐在一起喝咖啡——她是我辦公室裏的小姐，最近常常惹人厭。所以，我家裏可能出了一點小麻煩，請幫助我。——被誤認的案例

親愛的案例：

如果對你來說，這眞的是個難題，那麼你大可以刻意使自己看起來不具吸引力。去剪個難看的髮型，或穿上過時的衣服試試看。不過，我認爲一個三十歲的男人，應該有能力避免涉入他不想要的關係。讓對方知道你對她並沒有感情，這實在不是件困難的事。

解答➡ 1.（B） 2.（C） 3.（B）

A Willful Misunderstanding
蓄意的誤解

　　在午餐賓客隨時可能到達的時候，太太才發現家裏的麵包幾乎快吃完了。我建議讓六歲的小女兒凱茜，去店裏買一些回來。

　　「給妳一塊錢，」太太說道：「如果店裏有賣的話，就買兩條切好的三明治麵包，如果沒賣，就隨便買點東西回來，但一定要快喔！」

　　凱茜衝了出去，可是我們等了又等，最後才看到她跳啊跳的，走到轉角處，一個鮮紅色——而且很明顯是新的——呼拉圈在她的腰上轉來轉去。

　　「凱茜！」她的母親大叫：「那個呼拉圈是從哪裏來的——我叫妳去買的麵包呢？」

　　「是這樣子的，他們沒賣切好的三明治麵包——」凱茜答道：「——而且是你自己說，」她很憤慨地提醒我們：「如果沒賣，就隨便買點東西回來的啊！」

解答➡ 1.（B） 2.（C） 3.（C） 4.（D）

 Practice Without Pressure
在沒有壓力之下練習

　　有些運動員在私下練習的時候，都儘量把壓力減低到最小。這些運動員或是他們的教練，不讓新聞界參觀他們的練習，甚至拒絕爲了宣傳而發佈任何與練習有關的消息；這一切都是爲了保護自己，免除壓力。每一件事的安排，都希望能使訓練及練習的過程儘量輕鬆。結果，到了眞正比賽的緊要關頭，他們一點也沒有緊張的跡象，就像「冰柱人」一樣，對壓力無動於衷，也不擔心自己的表現會是如何。他們只是藉著「肌肉記憶」，做出各種練習過的動作。

解答➡ 1.（C） 2.（B） 3.（B） 4.（A）

63 That's Thin Enough
夠瘦了

當太太在醫師的指示之下，開始減肥時，這位住在新澤西州的律師感到非常高興。他太太身高五呎四吋，體重卻重達二百一十二磅，而且血壓高得驚人。

在十個月之內，律師的太太搖身一變，不但身材玲瓏有致，而且嫵媚動人。律師高興得不得了，就帶她去紐約市買毛皮大衣。很不巧的是，店員對她的美貌也心儀不已，他趁著幫這位太太試穿大衣的機會，雙手不斷地撫摸她的肩膀。

律師對自己的太太如此令男人心動，感到很憤怒，於是堅持要太太停止減肥，「你夠瘦了！」他這麼說，然後就開始帶她上昂貴的館子，享用豐盛的晚餐。直到太太的體重又回升到二百九十九磅時，他才善罷干休。

解答➡ 1.（C） 2.（A） 3.（C） 4.（B）

64 Spare the Rod…?
不打就…？

父親從來沒打過我們，我不知道他這種做法是否跟鄰居們不一樣；不過我們有一位遠親，名字叫威利，他非常勇敢也非常虔誠，但打起他的小孩來卻是一點也不留情。父親很遺憾他如此嚴厲，經常提起一件事：某一天，他跟威利以及另外一個人，從教堂走回家，他們談論到自己的孩子時，那個朋友轉身對威利說：「別在怒氣之下毆打孩子，先等一等，也許你就會改變主意。」我父親覺得這些話很有道理，經常一說再說，可是威利仍然照打不誤，原因是什麼，我也不清楚，或許是一種恐懼吧；也許威利認為，如果不把罪惡從孩子身上驅逐出去，將來他們可能會有什麼不測。

解答➡ 1.（B） 2.（B） 3.（A） 4.（A）

A Practical Suggestion
實際的建議

有一個老闆爲了讓員工有最好的工作環境，不惜花費了大筆金錢。

「現在，我希望每次我踏進工廠，」他說：「都能看到每個人高興地在工作；因此，如果你們有任何建議，能幫助我達成這個目標，請放進這個箱子裏。」

一個星期之後，箱子打開了，裏面只有一張紙條，上面寫著：「進工廠時，請別穿膠鞋。」

解答➡ 1.（B）　2.（A）　3.（A）　4.（C）

Training Elephants
訓練大象

訓練大象有兩種主要的方法，我們可以分別稱爲嚴厲的方法與溫和的方法。

前者就是讓大象去工作，不斷地打牠，直到牠按人所要求的去做爲止。即使不考慮道德的因素，這種訓練方法還是很愚蠢，因爲這樣會使動物心中充滿了仇恨，到後來說不定會憤而殺人。

溫和的訓練方法，在訓練的早期，必須對動物很有耐心，但是這樣卻能訓練出愉快、脾氣好的大象，能忠心耿耿地爲人們服務許多年。

解答➡ 1.（A）　2.（D）　3.（D）　4.（C）

Watch Closely !
仔細觀察！

爲了教導學生觀察的重要性，教授準備了一杯煤油、芥末和蓖麻油的混合液，他叫學生們注意看，然後先用手指沾一沾這杯噁心的液體，再舔一舔他的手指。接下來，他叫學生把這杯東西傳下去，讓每個人都依樣畫葫蘆照做一次，結果每一個人的嘴裏，都有一股噁心的味道。

在杯子傳回來之後，教授觀察每個人的臉，然後說：「各位先生，恐怕你們根本沒把觀察力派上用場，我放進杯子裏，跟放進嘴裏的，根本不是同一根手指。」

解答➡ 1.（C）　2.（B）　3.（C）　4.（C）

Over - Motivation
動機過強

如果人們在房子著火時，才去學習正確的逃生路線，所花的時間通常是沒有火災發生時的兩、三倍。有些人甚至學不會，因為在這個時候，動機過度強烈，因而阻礙了推理的過程。自主反應機構也會停頓，因為人們做了太多有意識的努力——他們努力過了。一種類似「蓄意顫抖」的反應會出現，而思考的能力也顯然喪失了。那些設法逃離火場的人，已經把自己的反應侷限住；如果他們置身另一棟建築物、或是稍微不同的環境中，他們的反應，還是會跟第一次一樣糟。

解答➡ 1.（B）　2.（D）　3.（B）　4.（D）

Mayan Mathematics
馬雅人的數學

墨西哥地區馬雅人的數學，比起其他較文明的文化，要高明了許多。在互行中東沙漠的阿拉伯商隊，將「○」的觀念帶到歐洲之前一千年，馬雅人對這個概念就已經很熟悉了。

希臘人用字母來書寫數字；而羅馬人的數字系統則極為複雜，要寫四個數字，才能把八（Ⅷ）表達出來。希臘人與羅馬人都無法像馬雅人一樣，輕輕鬆鬆地表達出大數目。相形之下，馬雅人只要用三種符號：點、直線或橫線，以及貝殼狀的○，就能把任何數目表達出來。

解答➡ 1.（D）　2.（D）　3.（C）　4.（A）

A Heroic Nurse
勇敢的護士

克蕾拉・路薏絲・馬斯是一位護士，她對於本世紀初黃熱病的研究，貢獻良多。當時她是一位平民護士，在古巴工作；陸軍少校威廉・高爾格斯和瓦特・瑞德也在古巴進行實驗，想隔離黃熱病的病因。實驗的結果，排除了污垢跟衛生不良是黃熱病病因的假設，而發現蚊子是可能的傳染媒介。克蕾拉當時自願被蚊子叮咬，後來她感染上黃熱病，在一九〇一年八月二十四日過世。在那次的實驗當中，她是唯一的女性，也是少數幾位因該病死亡的志願者之一。她一死，研究就結束了；實驗的結果證明：蚊子就是黃熱病的導因。

解答➡ 1.（A）　2.（D）　3.（C）　4.（C）

 The Disco-Dancing Parliamentarian
跳迪斯可的國會議員

路透社羅馬報導——義大利副總理吉阿尼・廸米契利斯，大力推薦緊張過度的從政者及商人們去跳迪斯可。

「不管是經理、老師、從政者…，每個人都得放鬆自己。有些人熱衷於高爾夫球，而我則對跳舞深具信心，」這位副總理上星期如此告訴記者們。

最近，他在義大利東海岸，一處他最喜歡的度假勝地大顯舞技。這位副總理在舞池中表現出過人的精力，助手們表示這是不斷練習的成果。他在兩個跳舞的俱樂部中，隨著強烈的節拍旋轉、拍手，一直到凌晨六點。隨後他在公務專機上打瞌睡，趕著去參加十一點在羅馬舉行的內閣會議。為了對抗緊張，廸米契利斯推薦「一劑良藥」——一星期跳一小時的舞兩次。「我們這些從政的人，腦子裏總是推滿了大小事情，所以我們必須放鬆，必須去跳舞，」他如此解釋。

解答➡ 1.（A）　2.（D）　3.（B）　4.（A）

Irrational Fears
非理性的恐懼

　　假設有個小孩在閣樓上玩，不小心把自己鎖在杉木箱裏，而出不來。他害怕得大叫求救，可是沒有人聽見，結果他在窄小的黑暗中被關了好幾個小時，一直到吃飯時，大家注意到他不見了，這才找到他。

　　二十年後，他可能已經把那個大木箱，以及被關在箱子裏的那段時間忘得一乾二淨了，可是每當他在電話亭中、在黑漆漆的衣櫥裏或是躺在火車的臥舖上時，一種莫名的恐懼就會湧上心頭；這種恐懼感既不合理，又無法解釋，但却是非常眞實又強烈的。我們的情感系統有某種方法，可以牢記我們已經遺忘的事物。

解答➡ 1.（B）　2.（B）　3.（D）　4.（B）

Modern Attitudes Toward Marriage
現代人對婚姻的態度

　　現代夫婦最害怕的就是承諾。不論是對配偶，或是某個機構，他們都不願意做承諾。

　　維拉諾瓦大學諮商及人際關係教授蕾結·哈爾瑪斯丁說，對八〇年代想結婚的男女而言，承諾這兩個字的意義已經不同了。她說：「承諾並不是指永不分離，而是指在雙方都願意的情況下，生活在一起。」

　　但是另外一位婚姻顧問則說：「想維持婚姻，唯一的辦法就是全心投入。如果你認爲婚姻不會永恒持久，那麼你的婚姻一定不順遂。因爲這樣的婚姻會變得乏善可陳。」

　　他還說，不幸的是，今天的夫婦就是無法信任婚姻；而這種不信任，竟然是統計數字造成的。

解答➡ 1.（A）　2.（D）　3.（A）　4.（D）

分析➡ until death do us part 相當於 until death parts us（直到死才分離）。當新人在教堂結婚時，牧師會問："Will you love

and care for … until death do you part?"，而新人則回答
"Yes"，或"I do"，或者重述牧師所說，"…until death
do us part"。

分析➡ they get that from the statistics 中，they 是指 couples,
而 that 則指 not to trust marriage。

Social Maturity
成熟的社會人

　　一個成熟的社會人，在任何場合中，跟任何類型的人，都能處得很好。
他不一定喜歡或尊敬所有的人；但是他心胸寬大，能體諒別人，又不會刻
意去傷害他人的感情。他也不會因為人們的種族、宗教、國籍、社會地位
或經濟狀況而心存歧視。

　　兒童和青少年常會表現出一副要獨佔朋友的姿態。但成熟的社會人
絕不會要求朋友，把全部注意力放在他身上；對於朋友的朋友，他也不會
嫉妒。

　　然而，他的感情卻是強烈而又持久的，因為他不會在發現朋友的缺點
時，就完全地失望。縱然他喜歡朋友的陪伴，而不喜歡孤單，但是在獨處
的時候，他也能娛樂自己，讓自己高興。

解答➡ 1.（D）　2.（A）　3.（B）　4.（B）

Our Works Reveal What Our Masks Conceal
觀其事知其人

　　觀其事知其人。在社交生活中，人們給你的是他希望這個世界接受的
表面，而你只能從他一些毫無知覺的小動作，一些他毫不知情、一飛即逝
的臉部表情來推論，才能真正瞭解這個人。有些時候，人們把自己所戴的
假面具發揮到淋漓盡致，以至於假以時日，他們真的與外表合而為一。但
是在他的著作或繪畫中，真正的他會毫不設防地表達出來；矯飾只會暴露

出他內在的空洞，任何特立獨行的偽裝，都無法掩飾一顆再平凡不過的心。在敏於觀察者的眼中，任何人最不經意的創作，都會揭露他心靈深處的秘密。

解答➡ 1.（D）　2.（B）　3.（D）　4.（C）

分析➡ Sometimes people <u>carry</u> to *such* perfection <u>the mask</u>

（ *that* ） *they have assumed* *that* ～

「有時，人們把自己所戴的假面具發揮到淋漓盡致，以至於～」

Dear Ann Landers

Controversy Over Breast-Feeding
對當眾餵母奶的爭議

親愛的安・蘭德絲：

　　八月時，我在內布拉斯加州，北普萊特的一份報紙上，讀到一篇文章，上面討論到愛荷華州杜波克市的一項新法令。這項法令禁止婦女在公共場所餵母奶，把餵奶時露出乳頭視為非法行為。

　　究竟是什麼不正常的心理作祟，使得這些人把餵母奶這種自然、充滿母愛的行為，當作色情？每當我看見一個婦女在餵母奶，我就看見了她對嬰兒的愛。

　　另外，我實在搞不懂，婦女無論何時露出胸部，有什麼值得大驚小怪的？乳房並不是性器官，它們只不過是富含乳腺的脂肪組織罷了。

　　　　　　　　　　　　　　　　　　　　　　　　──W.C.L.B.

親愛的W.C.L.B.：

　　我同意你的看法，婦女餵小孩母奶既不色情，也不是無禮的舉動；但是有些人看法不同，就會覺得不高興。所以，如果可能的話，最好還是避免在公共場所餵母奶。

解答➡ 1.（C）　2.（A）　3.（A）

心得筆記欄

||||||||||||| ●學習出版公司門市部● |||||||||||||||

臺北地區：臺北市許昌街 10 號 2 樓 TEL：(02)2331-4060・2331-9209
台中地區：台中市綠川東街 32 號 8 樓 23 室
　　　　　TEL：(04)223-2838

|||||||||||||||||||||||||||||||||||||||||||||||

英文趣味閱讀測驗③

編　　著／陳 瑠 琍
發　行　所／學習出版有限公司　　　　☎ (02) 2704-5525
郵 撥 帳 號／0512727-2 學習出版社帳戶
登　記　證／局版台業 2179 號
印　刷　所／裕強彩色印刷有限公司
台 北 門 市／臺北市許昌街 10 號 2 F　　☎ (02) 2331-4060・2331-9209
台 中 門 市／台中市綠川東街 32 號 8 F 23 室　☎ (04) 223-2838
台灣總經銷／紅螞蟻圖書有限公司　　　☎ (02) 2799-9490・2657-0132
美國總經銷／Evergreen Book Store　　☎ (818) 2813622

售價：新台幣一百二十元正
2000 年 9 月 1 日一版五刷

ISBN 957-519-259-1